797,885 Books
are available to read at

Forgotten Books

www.ForgottenBooks.com

Forgotten Books' App
Available for mobile, tablet & eReader

ISBN 978-0-243-50027-7
PIBN 10801885

This book is a reproduction of an important historical work. Forgotten Books uses state-of-the-art technology to digitally reconstruct the work, preserving the original format whilst repairing imperfections present in the aged copy. In rare cases, an imperfection in the original, such as a blemish or missing page, may be replicated in our edition. We do, however, repair the vast majority of imperfections successfully; any imperfections that remain are intentionally left to preserve the state of such historical works.

Forgotten Books is a registered trademark of FB &c Ltd.
Copyright © 2017 FB &c Ltd.
FB &c Ltd, Dalton House, 60 Windsor Avenue, London, SW19 2RR.
Company number 08720141. Registered in England and Wales.

For support please visit www.forgottenbooks.com

1 MONTH OF FREE READING

at

www.ForgottenBooks.com

By purchasing this book you are eligible for one month membership to ForgottenBooks.com, giving you unlimited access to our entire collection of over 700,000 titles via our web site and mobile apps.

To claim your free month visit: www.forgottenbooks.com/free801885

* Offer is valid for 45 days from date of purchase. Terms and conditions apply.

English
Français
Deutsche
Italiano
Español
Português

www.forgottenbooks.com

Mythology Photography **Fiction**
Fishing Christianity **Art** Cooking
Essays Buddhism Freemasonry
Medicine **Biology** Music **Ancient Egypt** Evolution Carpentry Physics
Dance Geology **Mathematics** Fitness
Shakespeare **Folklore** Yoga Marketing
Confidence Immortality Biographies
Poetry **Psychology** Witchcraft
Electronics Chemistry History **Law**
Accounting **Philosophy** Anthropology
Alchemy Drama Quantum Mechanics
Atheism Sexual Health **Ancient History**
Entrepreneurship Languages Sport
Paleontology Needlework Islam
Metaphysics Investment Archaeology
Parenting Statistics Criminology
Motivational

Notes / Notes techniques et bibliographiques

st original
opy which
lter any of
ich may
lming are

L'Institut a microfilmé le meilleur exemplaire qu'il lui a été possible de se procurer. Les détails de cet exemplaire qui sont peut-être uniques du point de vue bibliographique, qui peuvent modifier une image reproduite, ou qui peuvent exiger une modification dans la méthode normale de filmage sont indiqués ci-dessous.

- [ ] Coloured pages / Pages de couleur
- [ ] Pages damaged / Pages endommagées
- [ ] Pages restored and/or laminated / Pages restaurées et/ou pelliculées
- [x] Pages discoloured, stained or foxed / Pages décolorées, tachetées ou piquées
- [ ] Pages detached / Pages détachées
- [x] Showthrough / Transparence
- [ ] Quality of print varies / Qualité inégale de l'impression
- [ ] Includes supplementary material / Comprend du matériel supplémentaire
- [ ] Pages wholly or partially obscured by errata slips, tissues, etc., have been refilmed to ensure the best possible image / Les pages totalement ou partiellement obscurcies par un feuillet d'errata, une pelure, etc., ont été filmées à nouveau de façon à obtenir la meilleure image possible.
- [ ] Opposing pages with varying colouration or discolourations are filmed twice to ensure the best possible image / Les pages s'opposant ayant des colorations variables ou des décolorations sont filmées deux fois afin d'obtenir la meilleure image possible.

e manque

n couleur

) /
noire)

tion along
auser de
la marge

ay appear
ave been
ies pages
auration
cela était

The copy filmed here has been reproduced thanks to the generosity of:

McMaster University
Hamilton, Ontario

The images appearing here are the best quality possible considering the condition and legibility of the original copy and in keeping with the filming contract specifications.

Original copies in printed paper covers are filmed beginning with the front cover and ending on the last page with a printed or illustrated impression, or the back cover when appropriate. All other original copies are filmed beginning on the first page with a printed or illustrated impression, and ending on the last page with a printed or illustrated impression.

The last recorded frame on each microfiche shall contain the symbol → (meaning "CONTINUED"), or the symbol ▼ (meaning "END"), whichever applies.

Maps, plates, charts, etc., may be filmed at different reduction ratios. Those too large to be entirely included in one exposure are filmed beginning in the upper left hand corner, left to right and top to bottom, as many frames as required. The following diagrams illustrate the method:

| 1 | 2 | 3 |

L'exemplaire filmé fut reproduit grâce à la générosité de:

McMaster University
Hamilton, Ontario

Les images suivantes ont été reproduites avec le plus grand soin, compte tenu de la condition et de la netteté de l'exemplaire filmé, et en conformité avec les conditions du contrat de filmage.

Les exemplaires originaux dont la couverture en papier est imprimée sont filmés en commençant par le premier plat et en terminant soit par la dernière page qui comporte une empreinte d'impression ou d'illustration, soit par le second plat, selon le cas. Tous les autres exemplaires originaux sont filmés en commençant par la première page qui comporte une empreinte d'impression ou d'illustration et en terminant par la dernière page qui comporte une telle empreinte.

Un des symboles suivants apparaîtra sur la dernière image de chaque microfiche, selon le cas: le symbole → signifie "A SUIVRE", le symbole ▼ signifie "FIN".

Les cartes, planches, tableaux, etc., peuvent être filmés à des taux de réduction différents. Lorsque le document est trop grand pour être reproduit en un seul cliché, il est filmé à partir de l'angle supérieur gauche, de gauche à droite, et de haut en bas, en prenant le nombre d'images nécessaire. Les diagrammes suivants illustrent la méthode.

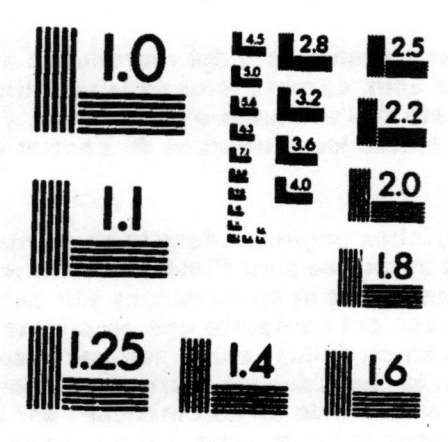

(ANSI and ISO TEST CHART No 2)

ELIZABETH'S PRISONER

McClelland & Goodchild's New Fiction

THE SPLIT PEAS   By Headon Hill

Headon Hill writes sensation stories, mystery stories, and stories of thrilling adventure that make the blood tingle in your veins. "The Split Peas" is a capital story of plot and counterplot, and love and patriotism. $1.25 net

THE PASSION OF KATHLEEN DUVEEN   By L. T. Meade

The love adventures of an extravagant young Irish aristocrat, Dominic O'Ferrel, who marries an heiress to enable him to pay his debts, form the backbone of a story abounding in incident. $1.25 net

THE EYES OF ALICIA   By Charles E. Pearce

A story of a crime and a mystery. Charles E. Pearce constructs ingenious problems which baffle all amateur attempts at their solution, and make a well-sustained and enthralling story. $1.25 net

THE SILENT CAPTAIN   By May Wynne

A tale of old France and the struggles of the Hugenots. In one of the most interesting settings of all history, May Wynne tells a romantic story of war and love. $1.25 net

ELIZABETH'S PRISONER   By L. T. Meade

A tale of moorland life in which a girl's pluck and self-sacrifice in pressing danger bring her to disaster and suffering, but eventually earn their reward. $1.25 net

JILL—ALL-ALONE   By "Rita"

The atmosphere of this "Idyll of the Forest" is essentially that of the woods. It is the story of the development of a young girl brought up by a hermit in the forest, till into her artlessness comes the awakening of love. $1.25 net

ELIZABETH'S PRISONER

BY

L. T. MEADE

AUTHOR OF
"THE PASSION OF KATHLEEN DUVEEN," "LOVE'S CROSS ROADS," ETC., ETC.

"I have you fast in my fortress,
   And will not let you depart,
But put you down in the dungeon
   In the Round-Tower of my heart.

"And there will I keep you for-ever
   Yes, for-ever and a day,
Till the walls shall crumble in ruins
   And moulder in dust away."
                    LONGFELLOW.

TORONTO
McCLELLAND & GOODCHILD
LIMITED

Printed in Great Britain

IN MEMORY

*Of one dearly beloved and never forgotten,
The friend and helper of the best part of my life.*

Because of the love I bore her, and because of her unselfish devotion and great natural genius, I give to one who no longer requires any earthly appreciation this little book. With much love, to

MARY MACLEOD

L. T. MEADE

ELIZABETH'S PRISONER

CHAPTER I

On the great moor of Hartleypool, the fog lay heavy. Folds of steam-like mist kept the barren, rugged landscape, with its innumerable hills and dales, waxing and waning continually before the human eye. At times the iron pile of the vast triple-walled prison would loom forward in bold outline, but a moment later it would fade into utter darkness as though it did not exist.

This heavy fog was quite common in winter at Hartleypool. It came early in the winter and stayed on until the beginning of spring. As a rule, it came at a moment's notice. Just now it was particularly aggravating, for an escaped convict was being hunted for. It was whispered that the man was a gentleman by birth, but he was only known in the prison by his number. His real name was, however, Adrian Trent. How he managed to escape no one knew, no one could guess.

He was supposed to be safe in his cell one evening, but by the morning he was away.

The jailor whose business it was to cast a bull's-eye light on every man under his charge, could have sworn that he was lying on his hard bed as usual all night—his head turned away, it is true, from the glare of the cruel bull's-eye—but his figure, a very powerful figure, stretched out as usual under the heavy bedclothes, and his head wrapped over by the coarse blankets; but, lo and behold, when the bitter morning dawned, and the fog lay thick on the land, there was only a bundle of clothes on the bed, and, in short, the bird had flown. He had gone out into the blackness which was neither day nor night, and all that could be done was being done to bring the poor wretch back to captivity. The man was a life prisoner, and his crime was murder. Warders and civil guards from the enormous convict prison searched the wide chasms and high hills of Hartleypool for a radius of at least twelve miles. Bloodhounds were imported to track the runaway, but as the days went by the scent got too stale, and the great dogs were pronounced useless to effect their object.

Adrian Trent was still at large. He was a strongly, well-built man, not more than twenty-four years of age. His height was a little over six feet; his shoulders were very broad. He was so admirably proportioned that not even the prison clothes could quite destroy his somewhat remarkable identity. His complexion was dark, but his eyes were very keen and intensely blue, blue as a summer's night, with thick long black lashes. His black hair was cropped close to his well-shaped head, and he wore the distinctly marked clothes of the prisoner, with the terrible broad arrow over everything.

There seemed no possibility of the man eventually escaping, nevertheless, he could not be found. The fog was very much in his favour, and equally against those who hunted for him. On this particular night the fog lay thicker than ever. It was at once like a wall; damp and cold like a river. At every possible road, at every possible turning, warders and civil guards were placed in twos and threes, in order to prevent the felon from escaping. " Starvation must do the business," said Captain Marshall, governor of the prison.

But notwithstanding every effort, the days went by and the nights went by, and the hunted man was still at large. It was quite ten days since the night of his escape. Close to Hartleypool is a town, which here we will call Hartley. A few ordinary people live in it, but the greater part of the town is taken up by the officers of the prison. The people on the moors who lived in sheds and solitary huts were anxious, more than anxious—the mothers were terrified, the girls were told to keep indoors. The boys, on the contrary, were anxious to help in the search, but their mothers besought of them not to do anything so rash.

Each hour made the vigil more terrible for the hunted wretch, and yet the people who belonged to the moors—men and women alike—could not keep back their fear at having a felon loose in their midst.

Just beyond the great moor of Hartleypool, and between three and four miles from Hartleypool Prison, was a square, stone-built house, which went by the name of "Craig Moor," and was the only house of any pretensions in that neighbourhood.

In itself "Craig Moor" was as lonely and desolate a spot as could be found on the face of the earth. The house was quite shut away from public view by a thick plantation of trees —there was a short broad avenue, which led up to the old-fashioned dwelling, and here resided, year in, year out, Professor Beaufort, the well-known *savant*, his wife, a timid, very gentle-looking woman; and, of late years, his young daughter, Elizabeth. Elizabeth was between twenty-one and twenty-two years of age. She had a slight, small, but very well-made figure, alert, bright eyes, a beautifully-shaped mouth, very firm in expression, and an equally determined step when she walked. All her life long this girl had devoted herself with heart, soul and strength to two special passions. These she had been able to cultivate to the uttermost. She was an artist, and year by year her work was hung at the Royal Academy, and year by year it was sold there. But she was also a profound musician.

Elizabeth did not object to Hartleypool. It was the very place where her special talents could find most vent. The dogs, the shaggy ponies, the moor men, the moor girls, gave her the subjects she required for her painting. She had, a year or two ago, been left two legacies, and out of part of this money she had built for herself a small studio on rising ground, and about a quarter-of-a-mile from "Craig Moor." Here she had for her painting a northern light, and all the usual accessories for her work. Here she had also built, partly by her father's help, who delighted in his only daughter, an organ. It was a small organ, but very good of its kind. It had been built into the wall of the studio, because the master of "Craig Moor" declared that music disturbed his thoughts and turned aside the current of his mind, which dwelt for ever and for ever on the great things of the forgotten past.

Now Elizabeth could not live without music. When she was not painting she was composing on her organ, which was worked by electricity. She made a great deal of money by both of these arts. She put this money carefully away, and never spoke of it. Her bright eyes, her well-formed lips, her eager expression, would show to any person of discrimination that here was a girl of extraordinary talent.

She was now engaged on a fugue, which she had been asked to write by an organist for use in a great London church. She was also exceedingly busy over her Academy picture, which, in this special year, consisted of a group of ponies, rugged as the moor ponies always are, a girl, a man and a boy. They were grouped with extreme care. They stood out boldly, declaring what they were, and looking so alive that no one could pass them without comment. This painting was supposed to be finished, but there was plenty of time before it must be sent to the Royal Academy.

Between painting and music Elizabeth's life was very full. As a rule, she left home immediately after breakfast, took her lunch with her, and did not return on many occasions until it was time to dress for dinner, for although she could not paint by artificial light, she could work at her music.

Mrs. Beaufort did not miss her daughter The Professor was glad, fond as he was of her, to have her out of the house. It was quieter without this bright young life. Mrs. Beaufort was a singularly timid woman. She never opened a book with the exception of her bible and prayer-book. She spent her time, both winter and summer, either knitting or crocheting. She made innumerable shawls. What she did with them no one could tell. Certainly Elizabeth never inquired. Elizabeth felt only glad that her mother was of that quiet and reposeful nature.

But now the tenth day had come and waned, and Adrian Trent, the felon, was still at large. The fog was more like a thick wet blanket than ever. The newspapers were full of Adrian Trent. They said that by birth he was a gentleman, but that fact, if it was true, made it, in the minds of the moor men and moor women, even more terrible than if he had been one of themselves.

Professor and Mrs. Beaufort were seated in their comfortable drawing-room. The carefully trimmed lamp made a very bright light. She, as usual, was knitting. He was examining, with the delight of the scholar, a fresh supply of choice volumes which had just been sent to him from Hatchards. The Beauforts considered themselves poor, but they did not mind this fact themselves in the least—they only kept one servant, a rough moor girl called Hephzibah.

Elizabeth had taught and trained Hephzibah. She had made out of these unpromising materials a good cook and an excellent and clean servant. Hephzibah would have laid down her life for Miss Elizabeth—her master and mistress she did not care about—Elizabeth was all her world.

Now Hephzibah was very nervous with regard to the convict, and even Elizabeth could not quite tame her fears. Professor Beaufort had a passion for fresh air, and although the night was so raw and damp, he insisted in his masterful way on having every window open at the top, and the blinds pulled up.

By and bye, close on eleven o'clock, Elizabeth entered the room. She came in quietly and quickly. Mrs. Beaufort gave a gasp; she beckoned the girl to come to her.

"My dear," she whispered, and her whisper was more aggravating than the loudest speech, "I do wish you would *persuade* your father to use common sense. You don't know what I'm going through. Elizabeth, I feel nearly wild with fear. That awful convict, that murderer, is still at large, and it is sheer madness to have a light in the room, the blinds up and the windows open. I assure you, my dear child, I sit here and shake in my shoes. The man is a murderer, and is certain to attack us. I know perfectly well that we shall come to grief. Do persuade your dear father, Elizabeth, to be reasonable."

Elizabeth had a calm and persuasive way. She went over now and laid her white hand on the old man's shoulder. He was very much older than her mother. His silvery white hair hung low on his neck.

"Daddy," said Elizabeth, in her clear tones, "mother is a little nervous about that poor convict."

The professor raised his head and looked into the eyes of his daughter.

"That poor—*what?* My dear child, don't interrupt me now, I've got a fresh meaning at last to one of the grandest passages in Euripides. It has long puzzled me. It has puzzled me for years, but its meaning has come now like a flash of light. I mean to write a paper on the subject."

"Daddy, the—the windows."

"The windows—oh yes, my love—anything in the world you please, only *don't* interrupt me."

With a smile Elizabeth crossed the room to

the first window. As she did this, two large, wild, starved-looking, dark eyes peered in at her from without, and at the same instant she perceived that pressed close against the glass was the face of a powerfully-built man. For a moment she even thought he held a small revolver, but eventually she discovered that he had only a stick in his hand. The professor was sitting with his back to the window, and did not, therefore, see the face of the man, nor the wild and terrible look in his eyes, nor did Mrs. Beaufort see any of these things, for she invariably sat as close as possible to the fire, busy with her endless knitting or crocheting.

Elizabeth knew well the art of self-repression. She needed it now. Without a word she made certain signs with her fingers. They were the alphabet for the deaf and dumb. She knew that it was the merest chance that this man should know the alphabet, but he evidently did. Without uttering a word she left the room, motioning the man outside the window to come to the front door.

When she entered the narrow hall, she saw Hephzibah there, crouching up and looking terrified.

"Oh, Miss Betty—darling—I'm that took with the shivers. Do you mind if I go straight up to bed. I feel as though the wretch is near—

close to me—but I'll be safe in my h'attic at the top of the house."

"Yes, go to bed at once, Hephzibah, at once. Don't stand staring, but do as I say. You have no pity for a starving man, who probably is dead long ago. But get into your bed in the attic, you'll be safe enough there. Here, I'll watch while you go upstairs."

"Oh, miss, miss—you know I'd die for you, but I can't help them shivers."

"Well, go to bed, they'll soon pass, it's a cold night."

Elizabeth stood quietly in the hall while Hephzibah ran upstairs and finally reached her attic bedroom, and bolted and locked the door, making a loud noise.

Elizabeth then, very gently, put the chain on the front door, and opened it about one inch. A figure was standing in the shelter of the little porch.

"You are Adrian Trent," said the girl, in a very low tone.

"Yes."

"You want to escape?"

"Yes."

"I will help you, but only if you'll do exactly what I say. You must remain quietly where you are until I come out to you. I may keep you waiting half-an-hour—no longer."

She softly closed the door and returned to the drawing-room. There she shut the windows and put the heavy shutters across and barred them.

"Elizabeth," said Mrs. Beaufort, "did I hear you talking to someone?"

"Yes, to Hephzibah," answered the girl. "She is so silly about that miserable convict. She says he'll certainly come and murder us all in our beds. Did you ever hear of such folly? I've sent her up to bed—the best place for cowards. And now, mother darling, won't you go, and also daddy? It is full time. I want to go over the house and shut it up everywhere, and I'm really very tired. I've been working so hard, both at my painting and my fugue, to-day."

"You do a great deal too much at your studio, Elizabeth," said her mother, "and now with that felon at large it is most dangerous. You ought not to go there until the wretch has been captured."

"Mother, there isn't the slightest fear, and, if necessary in the daytime, I can take my dog, Watch, with me. Now shall we all go to bed? Oh, I *am* tired. I can't lock up until you two have gone to your room. Do, do be quick, dears."

Professor Beaufort, when disturbed in his reading, generally got fretful.

"I never saw you so restless as you are tonight, Elizabeth," he said. "You have chattered so much, and come in and out of the room so often, that I've quite lost my train of thought. Yes, I may as well go to bed. I can do nothing further with Euripides to-night. Come, my dear."

The professor gave his arm to his wife. They both kissed Elizabeth and left the room.

The lonely house of Craig Moor was soon wrapped in slumber—that is with the exception of one person. When Hephzibah slept, it would take the blast of a trumpet to wake her. Professor and Mrs. Beaufort were both rather deaf. Elizabeth waited therefore until, by stealing a glance under their bedroom door, she knew by the darkness that the old people were in bed, and probably asleep.

Now was the time for her to make her own preparations—she had been thinking them out while she had been doing her best to get her family to bed. She peeped for a moment behind her blind and saw that the fog was denser than ever. She now tied up the light evening dress she had been wearing and covered her slim young figure in a long fur coat. She tied a red silk handkerchief round her dark hair—then, very carefully, she opened her door, shut it behind her, and went down stairs. There was one stair that creaked—she avoided it. Soon she was in the larder. She cut some cold meat from a joint put half a loaf with some butter and the beef in the basket. Then she added a tiny bottle of whiskey and a bottle of beer. The thing she next did was to select one of her father's great coats, one he had not worn for a long time and would probably never miss; she also chose a peaked cap to suit the coat. Her father was a tall, broad old man.

But now her most dangerous task lay before her, for she had so gently to open the front door that none of the sleepers in the house would hear a sound. With the aid of a feather and some oil she managed this, however. She put the door on the latch, looked to see that her own latchkey was on its chain, then stepped out into the murky, awful night.

For half a moment all was quiet, then a tall, broad figure loomed larger than the fog.

"I thought you had forgotten me," said a voice, a voice rendered harsh through suffering, yet still and notwithstanding, the voice of a gentleman. "If you had—if you really had—I am so desperate now that I would have forced my way into the house and taken food at any cost."

"Trent," said the girl, "do you wish me to help you?"

"You know it, Miss Beaufort."

"How can you tell that my name is Beaufort?"

"I have learnt the fact. I have watched you day by day, when you have not seen me. I thought from your look that you were the sort of brave girl who would help the desperate and despairing in the dark."

"I will help you, but I had to plan, and it took longer than I thought. Do you not indeed know me to be a girl without fear when I come out with you in the dark?"

"God knows my thoughts," replied the man, then he added, his voice changing to husky entreaty, "have you brought me something to eat? I've not touched food, except raw turnips, for so many days now, that I have ceased to count them."

"I have provisions for you in this basket, but you want something at once. Have a sip of this whiskey and eat a morsel of bread. Be quick, they may hear our voices. We must get out of this as soon as we can."

"Where are you taking me?"

"Where I believe you will be safe. Come now, we must walk quickly; I know every step of the road, even through the fog, but perhaps you do not, only you are weak owing to starvation. Had you not better put your hand on my shoulder, and let me lead you."

The man hesitated, tried hard to get a glimpse of the girl's face in the darkness. This he could not manage. He then laid his great hand with a faltering gesture, indescribably touching to Elizabeth Beaufort, on her slight shoulder.

"How strong you are," he ventured to say. "Imagine a great hulking fellow like myself leaning on you for support."

"Hush, don't speak! We have to walk a quarter-of-a-mile."

"My God, how my legs totter!"

"Come on," said Elizabeth. "Struggle for all you are worth. You will have a good feed when you get to your shelter."

They plunged together into what might have been called a wall of black night. Suddenly, when the man felt his last bit of strength had left him, the girl paused.

"Here we are," she said.

He could see nothing, the fog was so dense, and the dew lay like heavy rain on the lintels of the little house, or rather studio.

Elizabeth opened the door with a latchkey. She entered, accompanied by the man, then, very cautiously and quietly, she drew some heavy curtains across two shuttered windows. Afterwards she struck a match and lit a small piece of candle.

"This is the best I can do for you to-night,"

she said. "I dare not give you a fire, for the smoke might attract attention. This is my studio where I paint. These pictures are all mine. Now, do you see that sofa? When you have eaten and washed—I fear there is only cold water—you can lie on the sofa and put that big bearskin over you and—by the way, you are in your convict dress—that will never do. I have brought you an overcoat and cap of my father's. To-morrow I will bring you a complete suit of his clothes. He is a tall broad man —so are you. His clothes will fit you."

The man looked suspiciously round him. His eyes wore the terrible look of the hunted.

"Miss," he said at last, "I know that you are either angel or devil. Is this a trap? Have you brought me here to betray me?"

"To betray you, Adrian Trent, no! As there is a God above us, I have brought you here to save you. Only one thing, you must be guided by me. If you do exactly as I tell you, then you are absolutely safe."

"Is that a promise?"

She held out her firm white hand—the man half held out his own hand to take it, then he dropped it to his side.

"I must not touch your hand," he said.

"Why so?" she asked.

"I will do everything you ask me to do," he

continued, " but not that. Only believe that you have turned a devil into a man."

" Mr. Trent," replied the girl, " do not mind about touching my hand. You are not an ordinary convict."

" Ordinary enough," was the reply. " There are many like me in that place of hell. The fact that I am a gentleman and innocent goes for nothing there."

" I will save you," replied Elizabeth, with fervour. " The moment you spoke I knew you were a gentleman. Only the one thing I could not quite understand was why you wished to strike my dearly-loved father."

" I would not have touched him," said the man ; " I found a stick, and starvation had driven me—well—mad. But I know I could not have *touched* your father."

As he spoke he dropped his head on his hand.

" Now I must leave you," said the girl, " but I shall come again, ostensibly to paint, very early in the morning, and I will bring you then a further supply of food. Put out the candle as soon as you can, for although I do not think it possible, a chink of light may come through the shutters. Do not open them till I come. When daylight arrives you will find twilight through the chinks. You will also discover my favourite books on that shelf. To-morrow I have a plan to propose to you, which will make your residence here quite safe."

"My residence here?" said the man. "Surely, surely I may go further to-morrow."

"I am by no means sure. Remember you have promised to trust yourself to me."

"God above bless you, dear madam. I do trust you fully."

His hungry great sad eyes fixed themselves on her face.

"Put that candle out as soon as possible," she said, then she let herself out into the fog.

CHAPTER II

On the following morning Elizabeth Beaufort told her parents that she did not intend to paint at the studio that day.

The professor made no remark whatever, but Mrs. Beaufort expressed great satisfaction. She had been reading the local papers, and they were all full of the escaped convict, the general opinion now being that he was lying dead somewhere, his death caused by starvation, cold, misery and the fog. Still, means must be taken to secure him, dead or alive, so it was arranged that coraons of mounted police should scour the great moors, the hills, the dales, and that the numbers of armed civil guards and warders should be doubled.

The fog still continued. It was, in fact, heavier than the day before—the rugged, barren landscape dripped with moisture. It was dangerous for even those who knew the moor best to go far from the highway.

"I could not work at my great picture to-day," said Elizabeth, "so I have sent word to my models not to come. There is nothing to praise me about in not painting, mother, for I mean to occupy myself in other ways, and after I have done a little charitable work in the town of Hartley, I shall certainly go to the studio to get on with my fugue. I have a letter here from Sir John Archdale, asking me to let him have it at once, and such an order from such a man cannot be neglected, can it, father?"

"What, child, what?"

"Why, daddy, Sir John Archdale wants my work," replied the girl, with some little pride in her tone, which she had every reason to feel.

The professor rubbed his hand across his forehead.

"Yes, yes," he said, "most certainly. Get on with your work, Betty, work means—well, money—not that money is of the first consequence, but work also means the use of your brains—it means the joy of life. Go, Elizabeth, certainly, go by all means."

"But this morning," said Elizabeth, nodding to her father, her eyes brightening as she looked at him, "I mean to occupy myself in other ways. Hephzibah tells me that some very poor people of the name of Simpson have come to live at Hartley. There is a large family, and the father is in poor health. I cannot imagine why they have chosen Hartley, but they have done so. They seem, as far as I have heard, to be quite respectable, and I believe the man hoped to get work in the prison, but up to the present he has not succeeded. If he could get employment all would be well. I want to take this family a basket of food, and I want you, father, to give me some of your worn-out clothes. You know you have stacks of them in the wardrobe upstairs."

" Take whatever you like, my love," said the professor, just glancing up from his letters, then glancing down again.

Mrs. Beaufort began to murmur and complain under her breath, but Elizabeth was far too busy to listen. The night before she had made her plans. She went upstairs now, and selected from her father's old wardrobe, not only everything suited to a gentleman, but also some rougher clothes of a commoner make, which the professor sometimes used when he took a fit of gardening. These clothes were for Simpson.

Her intention was to go first to the studio, but she would visit the Simpsons later on. She invaded the larder and helped herself largely to meat, bread, butter, jam and beer, for she knew that she could not possibly visit Trent every day in his place of hiding; and yet, why not ? She surely had excellent reasons for going; both her music and her painting. Still, she could not possibly have her models round her. It was lucky that her Academy picture was finished, for she must give up painting for the present.

Accordingly, she filled a large parcel with clothes and a basket with provisions, then started on her way. The fog swallowed her up, as it did every living thing.

Mrs. Beaufort went by and bye into the kitchen, and relieved her mind to Hephzibah by grumbling about Elizabeth's queer ways.

"She has a dash of genius in her, not a doubt of that," said her mother, "but to walk all the way to Hartley in a fog like the present, is almost past belief. No other girl in the world would attempt it."

"Ah, well, madam," said Hephzibah, "ye could never moither nor lead Miss Elizabeth. Her always had her own way and always will. Her's the best and strongest lady in the world, but *ye* can't deal with her, ma'am, so don't ye try. Now there's Mr. Patrick, ye can come round *him* fast enough."

Mrs. Beaufort sighed and returned in a languid manner to her everlasting knitting.

Elizabeth reached the studio at a quarter to eleven. The convict had washed, had fed, had slept. He looked a new man.

"Now listen," said Elizabeth eagerly, "there are two rooms in my studio, one to the back, one to the front. The back room is used when I am in full work, for the horses and ponies and moor men and women and children. Kindly go in there now, change your clothes, and put these on, change everything. I know exactly where we can hide your convict clothes for at least a couple of days. Be quick, for I have a great deal to do and I must speak to you."

While the convict was changing his clothes, and getting into Professor Beaufort's neat and suitable garments, Elizabeth busied herself putting a great coat of varnish on her large Academy picture. The picture was completely finished, and did not need the extra varnish, but that fact mattered nothing to her.

" Now, Mr. Trent," she said, as a gentlemanly, quiet man came out and confronted her, " I have been thinking most carefully over everything, and I believe it to be most probable that you will have to remain here for a fortnight, at the most three weeks."

" My God, Miss Beaufort, you don't mean it ? "

" I do mean it ; I see no other possible way out. When the hue and cry has ceased, I can get you away disguised as my father, but that is for the future."

She coloured very slightly.

" Now please listen most attentively. In

order to make this place safe both for you and me, for please remember what an awful thing it will be for me if it comes to light that I'm hiding you here—don't shrink, please, I can manage. Now then, your attention. I am going from here to Hartley, the little town. From Hartley I shall go straight to the great prison. There I shall see the governor, Captain Marshall. I beseech of you don't look at me like that—I'm not going to injure you. I shall see the governor, who happens to be an old friend, and will tell him that owing to your escape I am too nervous to visit my studio and, in consequence, cannot get on with my work. I will further say to him that I would be exceedingly obliged, and very grateful, if he would send some of his officers with me, to have the studio searched. Have you a watch, Mr. Trent?"

He shook his head.

"How could I have a watch," was his remark.

"Of course you could not. Here, take mine."

She slipped it from its chain. Now, Mr. Trent, this is my plan. I shall arrive by and bye at my studio accompanied by the warders from the prison. I have not an idea how many will come with me, but most probably Captain

c

Marshall himself and a couple of his men. Now, do you see this great picture. It is wet with varnish. Do you observe this cupboard in the wall—this deep cupboard? The only entrance to the cupboard exactly fits the picture. I am going to put it there now, but before I do so, I want to let you into my secret. Behind the cupboard is another which can only be opened by a certain door being pushed into a groove, either to the right or left. In the inner cupboard I keep my bits of rags and all sorts of things that I need for painting. You observe that the inner cupboard is shallow, also that it is dark, but there is a hole at the top which gives ventilation. That hole is covered with tin filled with holes. Anyone standing or sitting in the inner cupboard would feel the draught and could not possibly be suffocated. Now I am going to put you into that inner cupboard, and will shut the door to. I will put also there your food which I have just brought, and all your convict's clothes. You can sit down if you like. You won't have much light, and you won't have anything whatsoever to do. After a time, perhaps after a couple of hours, you will hear voices. Those will be the voices of the officers who are searching the studio. I am going to pretend to be terrified about you. I am going to act the coward, so do not be surprised at any words you may overhear, only, whatever you do, Mr. Trent, stay quiet, for my sake and your own. You can eat some food before the officers come. You and your food and your convict dress will be hidden in the inner cupboard, and not a soul who is not in the secret will suspect that such a cupboard exists, or that there is anyone there. I have just re-varnished this great picture on purpose, and we'll put it exactly against the false door of your temporary prison. I will beg the police officers on no account to touch it, as they cannot do so without covering their hands with wet varnish and injuring my picture. That will sound very simple to them, and they will act accordingly. Now, Mr. Trent, I will ask you to go immediately into the cupboard. Are you certain that all your convict clothes are in this bundle?"

"Yes, that is all right."

"After the visit of the officers from the prison, this studio will be as safe to you as a grave. As soon as ever they are gone, I will let you out. You see I must pretend to be frightened."

"You could never be frightened," was Trent's reply.

Without another word he went into the inner cupboard. Elizabeth placed therein his convict clothes and his basket of food. She then slipped the sliding door to the left. In that position it looked precisely like a part of the wall. Her final act was to put the freshly varnished picture exactly in front of the door.

CHAPTER III

WHEN Elizabeth shut the studio door behind her, she took the parcel of rough clothes, which she had selected for Simpson and also some provisions for his family and walked as fast as she could through the ever-deepening fog to Hartley. She found the Simpsons' at home. Simpson was a soft looking man—perhaps that is the best way to describe him. He had shaggy eyebrows and long rough hair, his lips were thick and big, his whole appearance was of the sort that could not prepossess anyone. The man had tried in vain to get a post in the prison, but with such a face, such a personality, such an appearance altogether, nothing would induce the governor to give him what he wanted.

Accordingly Simpson was out of work, and accordingly he, his wife and three children were without food. Elizabeth's advent was like a ray of pure sunshine on this dismal day. The man was bending over the embers of a fast-dying fire in the miserable cottage he had taken. Elizabeth's bright presence was altogether a revelation to people of his class. He was not only roused himself but the neighbours clustered about.

Miss Beaufort coming to see the Simpsons! What could she want with them? They peeped in at the windows—they could not be got to move off. Elizabeth at last spoke sharply.

"I wish to see you alone, please, Mrs. Simpson. Ask your kind neighbours to go for the present."

Mrs. Simpson went out and said something. Whatever she said was efficacious for the neighbours slunk away. Then Elizabeth produced her father's suit.

"I am going to give you these," she said, "on a condition."

"And what be that, Miss?" asked the man.

"I want you to promise me n.   pawn them."

A cloud came over the rugged, yet weary face.

"Of course ye won't pawn them, Josiah," said the wife.

"No, no, I won't pawn them," said the man.

Then Elizabeth produced her food. The three children sprang at it like hungry wolves. There was beef, bread and butter and a small pot of jam.

Oh, what luxuries, what untold delights!

"This is your food," said the girl, "and I

hope you'll enjoy it. I am sure also you want a little money, so here are five shillings for you. Now I must go—I really must."

As Elizabeth was leaving the house she said to Simpson,

"You want to get work in the prison."

"That's what he has come about, Miss," said the wife.

"Well," said Elizabeth, "I am going now to the prison to see Captain Marshall. If you like to wear those respectable clothes I will say a word for you, Simpson."

"Oh, Miss, *ef* you only could."

"It'ud be the making of him, Miss," said the wife with her eyes full of tears.

"I will do my utmost—but, of course, I can promise nothing."

Then Elizabeth walked down the narrow street where the Simpsons lived and after a while reached the prison. On her way there she met a great cumbersome looking woman whom she happened to know, as she really knew almost every inmate of the town of Hartley.

Mrs. Heavyfoot now barred her way.

Mrs. Heavyfoot's husband was one of the warders of the prison

"How be ye, Miss," she said, dropping a curtsy, and surveying Miss Beaufort with eyes full to the brim of curiosity and venom.

Elizabeth knew well that her one object at present was to avert curiosity from herself — otherwise she would have taken but scant notice of Mrs. Heavyfoot — a woman to whom she had been systematically kind, but whom she honestly could not bear.

"It's wot might be called a real nasty day for a young Miss to be abroad," said the woman. "Fog thicker than ever — convict more despert than ever — but some Misses knows no fear."

"You are mistaken, Mrs. Heavyfoot," replied Elizabeth. "I can feel what I do not show. As a matter of fact," she continued, "I have come from home to-day on an errand of mercy. I did not mean to speak of it, but as you and your husband know all about the prison I do not mind telling you *in confidence, of course*, that I am anxious, most anxious, to get a berth in the prison for that poor fellow Simpson. I know he looks weak but that is caused by starvation — he is really a big, strong man, and when he can earn money sufficient to buy food for himself and his children he might be received by the captain. Of course *you* are with me in that, are you not?"

"Miss, I am not with ye in that, and what's more I never will be. Simpson, he's a skunk, that's what he be. Simpson — put in charge over *them men*—my word, Missie, you'm goin' on a fool's errand "

" I'm sorry to hear you say so, Mrs. Heavyfoot, but I can but try."

" And get nothing for your pains, Miss."

Elizabeth made no reply to this and a few minutes afterwards she was admitted into the prison. There was a small room not far from the principal entrance, into which she was ushered. She immediately asked to see Captain Marshall. He was in and Elizabeth waited quietly for him in the little room. How terribly dark and dismal it looked. She wondered at her own temerity. She was amazed at herself. Suppose everything failed. If the convict had left anything out by the merest chance both she and he would be ruined for life. How fearful, how terrible that would be! For a moment she almost wished she had never thought of her plan. However, there was no help for it now.

The next minute Captain Marshall, a fine, erect, soldierly looking man entered the room. He knew Professor Beaufort well and had met Elizabeth herself on several occasions. He admired her from the moment he first set his eyes on the open, young, frank face ; he greeted her with much cordiality.

" Well," he said, " what a wonderful day for

you to be out, Miss Beaufort. You are indeed a brave young lady to face the moors in a fog like this."

"I will tell you exactly why I have come to you," said Elizabeth. "In the first place I am not afraid of the fog, knowing all this neighbourhood so thoroughly as I do, but I have another fear, and I have come to you, Captain Marshall, about that."

"Indeed!" The captain drew a chair near the girl, sat down, and looked into her face.

It is this way," continued Elizabeth. "I am engaged, as perhaps you know, or perhaps you don't know, both in music and painting and have a great deal to do with regard to both of these occupations. I have a studio not far from home, where I both paint and compose different sorts of organ music. This fog, of course, makes painting impossible, but I have my organ built into the studio, and am at the present time working at a fugue. Fugues are used a good deal in church music. This morning I received a letter from Sir John Archdale, organist of St. Peter and St. Paul. He wants my work immediately. He wants it sent off to-day if possible, or at latest to-morrow."

"Well," replied the captain. He knew nothing whatever about music, although he loved it, but he knew the great cathedral of St. Peter and St. Paul, and he, of course, had heard of Sir John Archdale.

"I get very well paid for that sort of work," continued Elizabeth, "and this fact enables me to give my parents many comforts, which I could not otherwise bestow upon them. To be candid, I keep an open account at Hatchards for my father's benefit. He little guesses that I pay for his books, but the books are the delight of his life. In addition the work is a very great pleasure to me. Now, I've come to the point. I want to confess something."

"What is that, my dear young lady?"

"I never guessed it until lately, but now I know it is true. I am a sad coward."

"You—a coward!" The captain looked into the bright dark grey eyes, he looked at the stedfast mouth, he looked at the girl's thick dark hair—in short he looked at her from head to foot. She was slight, rather small, but the very essence of bravery seemed to shine all over her. Just for a moment it seemed incredible that a girl like Elizabeth Beaufort should fear any one in the world.

"I am a coward," she repeated. "I see you don't believe it. But I'm terribly afraid of *that* convict."

"What—Adrian Trent?" asked the captain.

"Yes."

"And why should you be afraid of him.?"

"I have a nameless dread that he has got into my studio and the fear has now become so strong that I have not ventured to go near the studio for several days. Each day I lose work, money, enjoyment. In consequence I am miserable, and last night the thought came to me that if you, Captain Marshall, would send some of your officials to my studio with me, in order to examine it, we should be able to find out if Adrian Trent was there or not. Once we discovered he was not there, my mind would be at rest and I should be able to undertake my employment again."

"Of course," said the captain. "That is a capital idea of yours. As likely as not the fellow *is* there. I shouldn't be a bit surprised. It astonishes me that we never by any chance thought of your studio, Miss Beaufort. Yes I will come with you myself and take a couple of men. We will drive there quickly with my blind pony. He goes just as well in a fog as in the brightest daylight."

"Does he really?" said Elizabeth in pretended astonishment, for she had heard this fact before.

"Yes, that's why I keep him. We have so many fogs at Hartleypool that I could not do without my pony and I would not sell him for all you could offer me. Now, shall we have a little lunch and then start!"

"But can we not start at once? It seems too early for lunch and I am anxious to get on with my work."

"We won't wait for lunch, then," said the captain. "I'll give orders for the trap to be made ready at once."

In a very few minutes the blind pony was attached to the little cart, two warders from the prison jumped up at the back and Elizabeth and the captain took their seats in front.

The captain took the reins and started off. The pony was told where to go and he immediately went in the right direction.

"By the way," said Elizabeth, remembering her promise to the Simpsons, "there is a family at Hartley in great distress. As a matter of fact they are starving and I had to take them food this morning. There are children and a wife and the man, Simpson by name, is most desirous to be taken on as one of your civil guards or officials or in any capacity. Of course, I must not press the point, but do you think he has a chance?"

"I am sorry—he has no chance whatsoever. The beggar has come to me many times and I have invariably told him the same thing. He is not the sort of person I want; I require a strong man, not a weak one. I want someone who will do what I desire without words, who will be *brave*. Why, Miss Beaufort, that fellow would let half the men in the prison escape. Now if *you* were in that class and a *man* and wanted work,"—he looked admiringly at the girl—she felt herself colouring slightly.

"You persist in thinking that I am brave," she said. "How little you know. Even now my heart is beating furiously."

"What—with myself and two of my warders to assist you and all of us fully armed. Ah, here we are at last. Well done, Tingo."

The captain patted the pony on his smoking flank.

Elizabeth took her latchkey, opened the door and they all went in. Then the search began. It went on and was soon finished. There was no trace of the missing felon. The captain desired his men to wait outside and take care of Tingo. They obeyed without question. He then looked at the really magificent picture behind which Adrian Trent was hiding.

Trent, with his heart beating very fast, was in reality at that moment within a few inches of the governor of the prison.

"What a really splendid picture," said Captain Marshall, "but let me tell you, young lady, you have it in a very bad light. I have not the slightest doubt I shall see it in the Academy this year."

"I hope so," replied Elizabeth. She spoke now with the utmost confidence and ease. "I am sorry, captain," she continued, "I would gladly put it in a better light for you, but I have had to varnish it, and the varnish is wet. If I should touch the picture now it would be ruined, but if you would return, say, in a fortnight's time, for the particular varnish I use dries very slowly, I will put it in a light where you will see it to advantage. The people in the picture and the ponies all belong to the moors. The poor people are so pleased to get employment, but now as I cannot gratify you with a sight of my picture—you can hardly see it at all in the dark—may I play something for you?"

She hardly waited for a reply. She sat before her organ, which was worked by electricity, and the next moment a magnificent volume of sound filled the little studio. The man behind the picture trembled from head to foot. He had been calm enough up to that moment, but now an unbidden sob broke from his lips.

CHAPTER IV

" By the way, do you suffer from mice here ? " said the governor of the prison, with sudden emphasis.

Elizabeth replied calmly :

" No—why should we have mice ? "

" I thought I heard them—or at least some strange noise—— "

" You are mistaken about the mice, Captain Marshall. The studio has only been built quite recently, and if we had mice I should certainly get a cat. Dear captain, you have greatly relieved my mind—we have searched everywhere--and the poor convict is certainly not here."

" Certainly he is not, Miss Beaufort, unless he is hiding behind that picture ? "

Here the governor laughed very heartily— as though he had found himself guilty of a very good joke.

Elizabeth laughed with him.

A few minutes later he said to her :

" Now I shall drive you home. It is hardly safe for you to walk alone in this dense fog.

As to that poor fellow Trent, I greatly fear he is dead. He could not live so long without food or warmth or anything of comfort."

"Do you really think he is dead?" asked Elizabeth.

"He is either dead or has escaped"

"Poor fellow, now that I know he is not here, I pity him; but I will not trouble you to see me home. The day is too dark for painting, but I can get on with my fugue."

"Very well, if you must, you must. Goodbye, Miss Beaufort. I will look in another day—did we say in a fortnight?"

"I think three weeks would be better," said Elizabeth.

The prisoner heard the governor drive away. The wheels of the pony cart, and the trot, trot of the blind pony grew fainter and fainter over the moor. Elizabeth waited until they had died in the distance, and then, most carefully and tenderly, she moved her picture, drew back the sliding shutter, and Adrian Trent appeared in view.

"What haven't you done to save me," he exclaimed, "but *why* did you play? You upset me there. That music—it brought back the days that are gone."

He fell on his knees, took her hand, and raised it, not quite, but nearly, to his lips.

"I ought not to touch your little hand," he said, "for I am defiled. O, my God, can you ever guess of what I am accused?"

"Of course, I know all about it, Mr. Trent, but then, you are innocent."

"That is true, but the law has proved me guilty. Guilty of bloodshed, of the most horrible murder."

"I know the story, *but* you are innocent."

"I was very nearly hanged," continued Trent. "Innocent or guilty, we must let that matter slide. At the last moment the Home Secretary gave me penal servitude for life instead—such a nice, such a kind exchange for an innocent man. A few months ago I was beloved. Society thought well of me, and so did my friends. I had a mother who, strange to say, never liked me, but whom I adored. I should not have undergone all the horrors of Hartleypool, but for her dear sake. I trust she is well, but I dare not inquire. Imagine, most pitying of women, what I have undergone."

"I will not think, nor must you. You have escaped, you are supposed to be dead. I mean you to escape absolutely, but it will take a little time. Now, as soon as ever the night comes you must shut these heavy shutters, but before doing so, draw down the blinds. Then, finally, you must draw these heavy curtains right across. After that you may light this lamp, which I am going to trim for you."

She did so, while he watched her eagerly.

"You may use the lamp," she said, "for two or three hours, not longer. First of all, however, I must prove things. See, I am going to draw down the blinds—now I fasten the shutters—now I pull the curtains across. *Now* I light the lamp. I mean now to go outside and see for myself if any chink of light gets through."

Elizabeth did so. She returned with a face full of joy.

"You are safe," she said. "You may read until you are tired. You have food enough until to-morrow. I am only very grieved that it must be cold, but I dare not light a fire. The smoke might betray us. Look at my bookshelf. You will find the sort of books you will enjoy."

"Why do you say that?" asked Trent.

"Because they are strong books, and you are a strong man. Don't interrupt me, for I know. I won't betray your secret, but you are suffering for another."

"How can you tell?"

The man's face turned ghastly. Drops of moisture stood on his broad forehead. Elizabeth took one of her delicate handkerchiefs and gave it to him,

"Take it and keep it, brave man," she said, in her brave rich voice. "Now I must go. If possible, I shall come to-morrow. If I do not come you have food enough. There is plenty of oil to refill the lamp. In short, you will know exactly how to act."

The forsaken convict gave the girl a swift smile of a sudden and most absolute sweetness. Then she went out into the fog, which was as thick and almost as black as night. Elizabeth felt intensely excited. It seemed to her that she knew the convict's unspoken story. She was saving a good, a great man, a man to be proud of, and by so doing, she was well aware that her own future was in extreme danger. If even yet he was discovered, if her daring deed was found out, it would be a case of Elizabeth Beaufort sharing the horrors of prison life with this man.

With a violent start she thought of the convict's clothes, which she had not yet destroyed. The burning of the clothes would cause a hideous smell, and as to the great awful boots, marked with Hartleypool prison on the soles, and also the broad arrow across the front of each, Elizabeth knew that her small fireplace would have little or no effect upon them.

She could, and would, burn the clothes by degrees, but the boots must be buried. There was no other possible way of getting rid of them. She hurried her steps. She might be able to visit Trent to-morrow. Yes, if possible, to-morrow she would bring fresh food. The Beauforts would never miss what she took from the larder. The Beauforts were the reverse of mean. In fact, they were very open-handed. They were also the reverse of suspicious.

Elizabeth liked to add all possible comforts to her prisoner's life. As she hurried home she thought of many dainties she might provide for nim.

All this time the prisoner was alone—no longer on that desolate moor. He had provisions, he had books, he had light. He had every comfort—a good sofa to lie on, the heavy bearskin to keep him warm at night, and all these things he owed to a girl—to God and this girl. What a strange, wonderful, brave, magnificent girl she was. He did not feel inclined to read. As the night came on the fog grew thicker and blacker, he drew the blinds, fastened the heavy shutters, and pulled the great curtains across the windows, then he lit the bright little lamp. He was in comfort, he was in clover. He ate a little, not a great deal, for after his long and frightful fast he could not manage to consume much food, then he thought of the books,

Elizabeth's books. He examined them. He was amazed at what he saw. Here were the choicest bits from German, French and English literature, here were books on music and on painting. There was no silly nonsense in this choice selection. The man took up one in particular. It was a book written in Italian, and was heavily marked. He happened to know Italian, and he found Elizabeth's notes as refreshing as the book itself. He liked to gaze at her clear, sharp handwriting.

Presently he put out the lamp, lay down on the sofa, and fell asleep. He fancied himself back at Cambridge, then he dreamt he was in the room with the Master of Trinity, and the master was talking of his mind—*his*—as something precious, a jewel beyond price. Ah, if he could see him now—a convict, escaping from justice and saved by a girl. *What* a girl! His sleep grew quieter. He ceased to dream the old torturing dreams. If he dreamt of anyone it was of Elizabeth.

Meanwhile, Elizabeth, on her return home, on the afternoon of that eventful day, was greeted eagerly by her mother.

"Oh, Betty, such news," exclaimed Mrs. Beaufort.

"What news, mother darling?"

"Patrick may be here to-morrow!"

"How do you know, mother?"

Elizabeth tried to keep an outward appearance of calm. If Patrick arrived before she had got Adrain Trent away from his place of hiding, all would be lost, for Patrick was a man who pryed into everything.

He was a very smart young officer in the Guards. He lived far beyond his means. He never came home except with the one object of getting money from his family. Elizabeth knew this fact well. As to the professor, he simply heard the news, made the sarcastic remark, "Pat always says he is coming, but he never comes," and went immediately back to work in his study.

"I am so happy," sighed Mrs. Beaufort. "I can't tell you what it is like, Elizabeth, but you will know when you are married and have children of your own. Ah, my Betty, a girl is a great possession, but a son—there is no one to a mother like a son! And he is so handsome, so striking-looking, dear fellow. We must get the place in perfect order for him, must we not?"

CHAPTER V

"Mother," said Elizabeth, after a slight pause, "what room do you wish Patrick to sleep in?"

"The usual spare room, I think," said Mrs. Beaufort.

Elizabeth suppressed a sigh of satisfaction. Mrs. Beaufort was so enamoured of her only son that she would have thought very little of desiring Elizabeth to give up her own room to Patrick. However, the spare room had a bigger bed and handsomer furniture and was also on the first floor. Therefore Elizabeth was safe from this danger. She went out by and bye to speak to Hephzibah.

"Hephzibah, Mr. Patrick has written to say he is coming."

"Written to say—" replied Hephzibah with a toss of her head. "Well, the poor missus will be in a state of delight, and then she'll be disappointed—bitter sore. I can't take to Mr. Patrick, I can't help it, Miss Betty. I can't help it indeed, Miss."

"We needn't talk about it," replied Elizabeth. "We'll just do what we can to make mother happy. Mr. Patrick often writes to say that he is coming and he doesn't come."

"That being so, it will be all the better for you, won't it, Miss"? interrupted Hephzibah.

"Why do you say that, Hepzie?"

"Oh, I has my own reasons," said Hephzibah.

She suddenly went up to the girl and took both her hands, she squeezed the two hands with vehement affection.

"Does ye think for a moment that I wouldn't be true to ye," she said. "Does ye think I wouldn't! Well, that's out! That's a load off me mind. I'd die for ye, Miss Betty, and I'd do nothing at all for Mr. Patrick, nothing at all."

"You are a good sort, Hepzie," said the girl. She did not dare to question the maid any further, but she felt absolutely certain from her words and manner that she had got a clue which she would not divulge.

The next day Elizabeth went early to the studio. She brought food in abundance for

played on her organ. This was what he liked best. She begged of him on these occasions to keep in the back room where he could not be seen by anyone who was passing the studio. She always kept the outer door locked and even visitors could not get in without her permission.

She was determined now not to admit anyone to the studio.

Day after day passed. Patrick wrote occasional brief notes, he even sent telegrams. He was very fond of sending telegrams, they were the most expensive means of communicating with his family, and, in consequence, he, being a poor man, adopted them. They did not need the trouble of composition, for they invariably said the same words,

"Can't come, mother. Possibly to-morrow."

The mother loved all these wires from her son, but as the days went by the imprisoned man became restless.

"I can't stand much of this," he said, "when can I go?"

Elizabeth looked at him out of her clear, true eyes.

"Believe me, I am preparing everything, Mr. Trent."

"Oh, I *am* ungrateful," he answered.

"But you must be patient," she continued. "The time will arrive when I can make all things ready for you, but it cannot be to-day or to-morrow."

Meanwhile Mrs. Beaufort was on wires with regard to her son. Patrick wrote, whenever he did write, to his mother, but at last there came a day when he wrote to his sister. He said in his letter,

"I feel that I must come very soon to see my mother, my father and you, Betty. My object in coming is money and money alone. Now, clearly understand that I want money and soon, very soon. I shall, therefore, in all probability, be with you at Craig Moor within the next two days. You and I can have long talks in the studio, and, of course, with your two legacies and the amount of money you must have made by your pictures and your music, you must now have a goodly pile. It is unaccountable to me how anyone can pay money for mere music, but anyhow, if you can make it—well and good. I shall, in all probability, arrive the day after to-morrow. This is real, this is earnest. Now be prepared to give a good haul out of your earnings to your poor Patrick, little sister, otherwise I shall be cashiered."

Elizabeth did not show this letter to her mother, but she knew that the time had arrived for her to make a distinct move with regard to the prisoner, Adrian Trent. Accordingly she took another suit of her father's clothes and in the dead hours of night she went to the studio. She had taught
knock which she gave on the door.

Trent was amazed when he saw her. She said to him:

"I mean to-morrow night at eleven o'clock to come away with you to London. I have made every possible arrangement. I am going to sell my horse, Swift-as-the-wind, and my trap, and I'm going to give you fifty pounds. Don't be too proud to accept it from a girl who feels that she has fulfilled a great mission in life in saving a man like you."

"Miss Beaufort, *how* can I take it?"

"You can, you must. Be ready at eleven o'clock to-morrow night. I shall not come to the studio earlier. I will drive you to Barleigh station, just six miles from here. I am going up myself about selling Swift-as-the-wind. You must wear these clothes and this wig. It will conceal your want of hair completely, and you will put on this old-fashioned cap of my father's. If anyone happens to see you, that person will think you are Professor Beaufort, but at that time of night no one will recognise you. With fifty pounds you can go to the other side of the world and start afresh. And now, good-night. Sometimes think of me, as I shall think of you."

"Good-bye," he answered. There was a choking sound in his throat. He could with difficulty contain his feelings.

Elizabeth left him.

The next day passed much as usual, but in the course of the morning Elizabeth told her parents that she was going up to London with her horse and trap, that she no longer needed Swift-as-the-wind and had written to Tattersalls to request some of their men to meet her at the station in order to take the beautiful creature away to sell him. She said she required a little extra money.

The professor looked at her in astonishment. Mrs. Beaufort said,

"I have no doubt the money you get for the horse will be useful for dear Pat when he comes!"

"Dear Pat!" echoed the professor. "Dear Will-o-the-wisp, who never appears, who always *says* he is coming. Well, my dears, go your own ways, but don't keep me from my studies."

Elizabeth did not tell anyone else of her intentions. Her one terror was that Patrick might arrive that day, but there came another telegram from him at noon again postponing his arrival. After that she felt happier and stronger.

The family went to bed as a rule very early and they were all sound asleep when the girl went softly to the stables. She took the horse out and harnessed him to the little dogcart which she generally used. She patted him on his proud and glossy neck, she kissed him between his eyes.

"Darling," she said, "I give up the best thing on earth when I give you away. Never forget me, Swift-as-the-wind, never forget Elizabeth Beaufort."

Then she jumped into the dogcart and a few minutes before eleven o'clock left the house, the rest of the inhabitants being sound asleep.

On the stroke of eleven o'clock she reached the studio. She scarcely recognised Adrian Trent in the loose old suit of her father's clothes which she had given him. He was wearing, in addition, a white wig which the professor had once worn in some village theatricals. She now took care to see that all the prison clothes and also the suit which the prisoner had worn during the time of his captivity were put safely away behind the hidden door, in front of which still stood the great picture. She then looked carefully round every scrap of the little studio. All was right. There was not a trace of the convict's residence here for nearly three weeks, anywhere to be seen. Anywhere — *except* behind the hidden door — Ah! yes—behind that door was evidence enough. But no one would look behind that door—Elizabeth resolved to burn all the clothes except the heavy boots to-morrow night—the boots of course must be buried.

She went up now briskly to Adrian Trent.

"Mr. Trent," she said, "you have behaved magnificently—but now your time for inaction is over—I think I have arranged everything—you are coming with me at once to London—you are disguised as my father—we shall reach London early to-morrow morning—then we must part as strangers—yes—as strangers—but listen—we have a few minutes to spare—I have bought for you a first-class ticket on board the *Lusitania*—for New York—you will have time to get a small outfit to-morrow—the *Lusitania* leaves Liverpool at an early hour on Thursday morning—so you had better go to Liverpool to-morrow night *at latest*—here is your ticket for the boat; I have entered you as Mr. Henry Councellor. Be careful to keep that name as long as possible. Now, with regard to funds, your ticket is paid for, *here it is*—You will want about twenty pounds to buy a very simple outfit—here is the money in gold—you will want money when you arrive at New York—here are ten five pound notes—take them and do the best you can with your new life."

As she spoke she closed his strong hands over the ticket—for America—the gold and notes—

"I never spent money so gladly," she said—then she added, "This is the proudest day of my life—yes—of *all* my life—God bless you—God keep you."

There was a distinct thrill in her beautiful, brave voice.

They drove in absolute silence to Barleigh. Barleigh had a later train to London than had Hartleypool. A porter was waiting for Elizabeth and her father. She took two first-class tickets—they were hurried into their carriage while the horse was put into an empty horsebox and the cart into the van. Instantly the train moved out of the station. Trent and Elizabeth were alone. The guard had locked them in, owing to a generous tip on Elizabeth's part.

As they moved out of the station, Elizabeth bent towards Trent—she touched him on his arm.

"You are free!" she cried. "Thank God for His great mercy, you are free."

"Free, owing to you," was his answer. He bent forward and suddenly and passionately kissed her hand. "Forgive me, oh, forgive me," he cried. "I know I can never, never do it again. I shall never as long as life lasts see your beautiful face again, but as long as I live, as long as I live, I will remember your wonderful, your marvellous kindness, and for your sake alone, I will endeavour, if possible, to mend my broken life."

"Do not say any more," answered Elizabeth. She spoke in a strangely troubled voice. "There is that in me," she continued, "which *must* help those who are in trouble. Think of it in that light and forget—forget all the rest."

"No, I can never forget," was his reply.

She turned a little away from him. He wondered if he had done anything to annoy her, but she did not show it in her calm, pale face.

During all that long journey to town the man who was now to call himself Henry Councellor kept his dark eyes wide open and fixed eagerly on the girl. She closed hers, wishing that she could sleep, wishing earnestly that he would not look at her, wishing above all things that her own heart did not beat so terribly fast, praying frantically under her breath that one so good, so noble, should escape. Yes, he must escape, he was worth saving. He was worth going into danger for. He would escape, she felt a certainty on the subject—he would—he must!

At last they reached their journey's end. Obeying her desires, for she spoke to him again, just at the end, Trent walked quickly away and mingled with the crowd. Two men were standing on the platform, ready to convey the horse and neat little cart to Tattersalls. It was possible that Elizabeth might buy another horse some time, but not now. She dragged herself wearily along, somewhat like a woman with a broken heart. She had been absorbed for over a fortnight in a scheme of extreme danger and peril. She believed that it had come off successfully, but a strange thing had happened, for during that period of almost three weeks of imprisonment in the little studio, whenever she and Trent were talking together, he had begged and implored of her to listen to his story, but she had absolutely refused.

"Better not," she said, "I know you are innocent, that must content you."

"If I might speak, just once," he implored.

"Better not," she replied again. She knew that his self-control was trembling in the balance, she knew that she must keep him and herself on guard. She was an intensely proud girl and never before had she felt for anyone as she felt for this man. She well guessed his feelings towards her, but he must not speak of them—she must prevent this at any cost. He must not speak—sentiment must be kept at bay. They would, in all probability, never meet again. That was her feeling, but as she took a taxi-cab and drove to the nearest hotel in the early morning, she knew well, she knew absolutely that she was *his* prisoner, quite as much as he was hers.

CHAPTER VI

ELIZABETH BEAUFORT, owing to her legacies, and also to the money she earned by her painting and music, had some hundreds of pounds in a London bank. This money she never spoke of, and none of her own people were aware that she possessed it, but from the precious store now, she had drawn sufficient to give Trent a very simple wardrobe, to pay his passage as a first-class passenger to New York, and to give him £50 over and above to start work.

Having drawn so largely on her funds, she felt she could not keep Swift-as-the-wind, and, further, her idea of selling the horse and taking him up to town by a midnight train in her supposed father's company made an admirable reason for getting Adrian Trent away. Now he was gone, gone for ever. How dreadful the studio would look without him. She could hardly bear to think of the desolate place. Her fugues and oratorios, her paintings—all had lost their savour. Suddenly, as she drove to a small hotel, a great fear went through her breast. How simply mad she had been not to make an effort to destroy the convict's clothes while the fog lasted. At any cost she would make it her first business that night. Elizabeth had worked her plans with such skill that she had not one confederate—confederates were dangerous.

Mrs. Beaufort imagined that Elizabeth would remain for a couple of days in London with an old aunt of her own. Elizabeth would have done so but for the convict's clothes. The old great-aunt would welcome her, and she would be glad to be away from Craig Moor for a few days, but now she knew well that she must return quickly home.

Mrs. Beaufort was in an unceasing state of worry about Patrick; Patrick was her idol, and gave her all the trouble that most idols do. Each day he wired to say he was coming and then, at the very last moment, wired to postpone his visit. His bedroom was in readiness, his fire blazed merrily, but the dearly-loved son had not put in an appearance. It was entirely on account of Patrick that Elizabeth hurried Trent's departure; she now sincerely hoped that he would stay away for yet a day or two longer, just in order to give her time to get rid of the convict's clothes. The clothes themselves, and the old suit belonging to her father, she could, with considerable difficulty, burn in her little grate, but the burying of the boots was another matter. How could she possibly dig a grave for the boots with Patrick hovering about the place. He found Elizabeth much more entertaining than his mother, and came to the studio at all hours and times.

Elizabeth arranged to take the *two* o'clock train back to Hartley. She wired to the station-master to have a cab in readiness for her, for she could not go to town without a very little luggage. What was her horror as she reached the platform at Waterloo to see Patrick himself pacing up and down, evidently waiting for her train. Patrick was a very tall and striking-looking man. He was always exceedingly well-dressed by a tailor who seemed never to expect to be paid. He belonged to a regiment of guards, and was one of the smartest officers in that crack regiment. He was now serving with his company at Whitehall, but sincerely hoped soon to obtain that delight of a man heavily in debt, an exchange into foreign service.

When he saw Elizabeth he gave a start of astonishment and came up at once to her side.

"My dear sis, what has brought you to town?"

She allowed him to kiss her; he was her brother, but she had no respect for him or his ways. Her's was the soul of honour. He did not know what honour meant.

"I'm running down to catch a peep at the old lady, sis—but, good gracious, Betty, whatever is the matter. How dreadfully white and fagged you are looking. Whatever are you, my little country mouse, doing in town?"

"I came up last night, Patrick, to sell Swift-as-the-wind, and as the cart is no good without the horse I brought it up also. They assure me at Tattersalls that I shall get a good price for Swift-as-the-wind—he is a thoroughbred, and I have trained him myself. I suppose," continued the girl with a sigh, "one sometimes has to put up with money instead of the creatures one loves."

"My dear, foolish Betty, there is nothing in the world like money. I do hope that Swift-as-the-wind will fetch a good price, for I'm coming begging, little sister mine. I gave you a hint of that in my letter. Oh, nothing to terrify you, my dear. Only when a poor chap belongs to a crack regiment, and is given a miserable pittance for his services, he can't live on it. But time enough for unpleasant matters. I have every hope that I may get my exchange, and if so, good-bye to creditors and all the abominations of a London winter. How is the mater, Betty—and is the gaffer as keen as ever over his research work. Good old chap—the gaffer. I'm proud to be his son. Over and over I've just mentioned that fact and got a fiver in consequence. For goodness sake, Bet, don't look at me with those shocked eyes. I can stay at Craig Moor for a couple of days—not much longer, for it is such a beastly hole. You do look white, Bet. I wonder what you've been doing with yourself—running away with that escaped convict, or something of that sort?"

To her intense annoyance Elizabeth felt her face flush deeply, and she also knew that her brother remarked it. His eyes twinkled with suppressed mirth.

"You are just like all women, Bet," he said.

"Oh, Pat, don't be silly—how could I get sentimental over a man I've never seen?"

"Then why did you turn like a turkey cock when I spoke of him just now?"

"I suppose I flushed a little because I was tired."

"Not a bit of it, my little sis," thought the astute young officer, but he did not speak his thoughts aloud. He turned the conversation to indifferent subjects.

The escape of Trent was the talk of the country. Was it possible that his sister had anything to do with it? If so, he would obtain a handle over her which might prove exceedingly useful, but he must be wary, and do nothing rash until he was sure of his ground.

Elizabeth, having been awake all night, was now so tired that she slept most of the way back to Hartley. Patrick watched her. He observed the noble cast of her young face. He saw that she was really beautiful, and he felt that under given circumstances, he might be proud of her. But his own financial difficulties presently occupied his mind. As a matter of fact, he was in a sore strait, and unless he could get considerable relief soon, ran a very likely chance of being cashiered.

Why was Elizabeth selling Swift-as-the-wind? His sister was supposed to be comfortably off. She lived at home for nothing and, as he knew, had been left within a short time two small legacies. He had hoped that these legacies would fall to him, but no such luck. What did girls want with money? Again he thought of the escaped convict. His heart beat fast. Elizabeth could be locked up —locked up for years if she had really aided and abetted an escaped felon, and, of course, there would be a big reward offered for the man. This reward would come in handy for Patrick, but, of course, he must be careful not to betray his sister. The first thing, however, was to be sure of his ground. He would question Elizabeth closely to-morrow on the subject of Swift-as-the-wind.

The brother and sister arrived in good time at Craig Moor, where Mrs. Beaufort received her son with rapture. He had a way of petting his mother, which was her delight. And before she retired to her bedroom that night, she wept bitterly over his troubles, said he might be certain of *her* last penny, and promised to broach the subject of Patrick's troubles both to the professor and to Elizabeth.

"Why, my boy," she said, "Elizabeth alone could put you right if she would. She must be simply coining money with her work and her legacies."

"That's what I think," said Patrick; he went to bed much cheered, and slept the sleep of the just, but Elizabeth was too canny for him. She managed to put a small dose of bromide of potassium into a stiff tumbler of whisky and water, which she brought to him just before he went to bed. Presently she listened outside his door. He was snoring gently and peacefully—all was well. She then crept downstairs and went once again in the dead of night to the studio. Here she drew down the blinds, fastened the heavy shutters, pulled the thick curtains across the windows, then lit her lamp and prepared a large fire—as large as it would hold—in the grate.

When the fire blazed freely, she drew back

the sliding panel of the cupboard and took out the convict's clothes. One by one she thrust them into the heart of the fire, and before long they were consumed. Then, with a pang at her heart, she also burnt the suit of clothes of her father's which the convict had worn.

Now all evidence against the felon was destroyed, with the exception of the heavy boots. She made up her mind not to bury these near the studio, but to bring them home, wrapped in a thick sheet of paper. She had a very large, old-fashioned press in her bedroom, which had been given to her by one of the aunts who had left her a legacy. She could hide the boots in the press until such time as Patrick had departed. She would then get rid of them in the depths of the forest, which, in certain parts not far from her home, fringed the downs.

She managed to go and return unseen, unmolested, and by three in the morning she got into her own bed. She felt at last tolerably happy, and did not think that Patrick could injure her. She did not know, however, that fresh troubles were ahead.

At breakfast the professor turned and spoke to her.

"By the way, Elizabeth, you took, a few weeks ago, some clothes of mine to a poor fellow of the name of Simpson, a man who, I believe, lives in Hartley. I wish you could manage to pay him a visit. I have no idea what clothes you took, but—what's the matter, Betty?"

"I dropped my napkin ring," said Elizabeth. "Yes, father, what am I to say to Simpson?"

"Ask him, my dear, if he found in any of the pockets of my coats or waistcoats a packet of letters from Professor Dale, of the Royal Society. I have lost them—they would be of no manner of importance to him, but are vital to my research, and I cannot really trouble Dale again."

"I'll ask him, of course, daddy," said the girl, with a sinking heart, then she added, "Is it likely, father, that you would put valuable letters into old clothes that I would give away? I know the clothes that I gave to Simpson—I gave him a very old suit that you used for gardening."

"As to that I cannot say," replied the old gentleman in a testy voice. "I only know the letters have gone, and you may just possibly have given clothes to Simpson not suitable for him to wear."

"Oh, I know what clothes I gave him," replied Elizabeth.

Patrick's bold, black eyes were fixed on his sister's face. He said:

"It is a great nuisance that you have sold

Swift-as-the-wind, but I shall not object to walking with you to Hartley."

On the road Patrick thought it best not to allude to the subject of money. He was extremely cheerful, and even kind, to his sister. He asked her how she spent her time. He kept on repeating that she was a lucky, very lucky girl. He sighed heavily as he uttered these words.

"Some people have luck," he said, "and you are one of them. But, Betty, I wonder you don't marry. Do you know, you are uncommonly handsome, and marriage is much more suited to a woman than any amount of so-called professional work."

"I am in no hurry to marry," said Elizabeth. "I don't know that I wish ever to marry."

"Then," said Patrick, with a laugh, "that is a sign manual that you will. Don't you know that you have a way about you that would attract any man. Of course, buried alive as you are here, with no one round you but convicts, what chance have you. Why, my dear girl, you can't even fall in love."

Betty laughed and wished Patrick would not turn and look at her so often. By and bye they reached the cottage where the Simpsons had lived.

Alas for the poor professor and his chance of

recovering his letters, the Simpsons were there no longer. They had migrated, nobody knew where, over a fortnight ago. They had taken all their belongings and had simply decamped, leaving their rent unpaid. Mrs. Heavyfoot, who gave Elizabeth this news, said that they were a good-for-nothing lot, and that the young lady was far and away too kind to them, giving them such handsome clothes and such money and all.

"The clothes were not handsome, they were quite worn," said Elizabeth.

"Can you tell me what clothes my sister did give them?" said Patrick.

"Oh, ay, that I can—I remember better than well," said Mrs. Heavyfoot, "because Eliza, their eldest girl, called me in after Miss had gone, to have a look at them. She said she only wished Miss had brought her some things for herself, but they were every one of them men's clothes. Why, that chap Simpson, that good-for-nought, he was set up for the winter."

"But what did he get, can you remember? Elizabeth, why don't you speak," continued Beaufort, "this is very important. You don't seem to care one bit whether our father's letters are lost or not."

The girl turned on him angrily.

"Of course I care, Patrick, and as I know

exactly what clothes I did give to Simpson, I don't see that we need inquire of Mrs. Heavyfoot."

"That's as you please, Miss," said Mrs. Heavyfoot, giving her great head a violent toss. "I'm sure I'm the last woman to interfere with my neighbours, but I'm glad them bad lot have gone, and that you didn't give 'em any more, with honest folks a-longing for 'em. Why, in course they'll only pawn them. 'Tain't likely a rough man like Simpson 'ud be wearing them good cloth clothes any length of time."

"Do you think the man has pawned the things here," asked Patrick, in an eager voice.

"No, sir, I never heard tell of it."

"The thing is more important than you imagine," said Patrick, "for my sister, in a fit of generosity, gave away a coat or waistcoat belonging to my father which contained a packet of letters. My father says the letters are exceedingly valuable to him, being on subjects which are of *no* importance *but* to him. You understand that, don't you, Mrs. Heavyfoot."

Mrs. Heavyfoot nodded; she did not understand, but it was as well to pretend that she did.

"I don't think that he'd pawn them here, sir," she said, "but you might enquire, there's no knowing."

"I don't want to go to a pawnshop," said Patrick, slightly dilating his delicate nostrils, " nothing of the sort for me, but if you would go, Mrs. Heavyfoot, I would give you——" here he spun a two-shilling piece deftly in his hand. At the same time he looked at the woman out of his brilliant eyes.

" Of course I'll go in a twink," she replied. " It's plain to be seen that a smart young gent. like yourself, sir, wouldn't be seen inside a pawn-shop."

The woman went, and while she was away, Elizabeth paced up and down in front of the cottage. She felt exceedingly angry with Patrick, and would have done anything in the world to get him to give up this absurd search.

By and bye Mrs. Heavyfoot returned. Simpson had not been to the pawnshop, there was no doubt of that.

" Then look here," said Patrick, " this is an urgent matter, and you will be paid just according to your success. Can you manage to track Simpson to his present abode. I think I can promise you that my father will give you a sovereign if you bring back the letters."

" My word, sakes alive! A whole sovereign!"

" I can't positively say, but I think so. Anyway, take it from me—you will be well rewarded, only you must be quick."

"I'll do my very best, sir, you may be sure of that. It seems hard that dear Miss should have been taken in, as it were, by people of that sort, but it were that gad-about Hephzibah who told her, I'm thinking. I don't take to Hephzibah—just a moor girl—no, I *don't* take to her although she be your servant, Miss. I wish you'd have a try with my gel, Julianna; Julianna is worth ten of Hephzibah, and honest as the day, which Hephzibah is *not*. She's always *spying* and *watching*, is Hephzibah."

"I won't have a word said against her," interrupted Elizabeth. "She is our servant, and we find her quite faithful. Now, I must wish you good-day, Mrs. Heavyfoot."

"Hoity-toity, however have I offended her," thought that good woman. "It's mighty strange, too, how that convict have escaped. I don't believe he'd have managed it if young master had come a week back. He's a fine figure of a man, is young master; why, it's a real pleasure to look at him. Miss is handsome, but she's not a patch on her brother, not a patch."

"Now, what shall we do," said Patrick, as they walked slowly away, "visit the prison and find out if there's any news of the convict?"

"Oh, no, Patrick, why worry ourselves about that poor fellow. I'm certain he escaped days ago, or—or is dead."

"You are certain, are you? I wonder why you are certain."

"It is only a feeling I've got. A man could not live, however strong he was, for over three weeks without food, and some sort of relief, in the middle of our black, cold, dreary winter."

"That's true enough. Well, I only hope he'll be caught yet."

"Why should you wish him to be caught, Patrick?"

"What can you mean, sis? Of course I wish him to be caught—a felon, a man who killed a girl. I read up the whole case. I'm always interested in murder cases. It seems that he and his brother were both implicated, and, in the first instance, circumstances were strongly in favour of the other man being the murderer, but all of a sudden, this one, Adrian they call him, *confessed*. He declared in open court that he did it, and in consequence Valentine, his brother, got off scot free."

This news was fresh to Elizabeth, and she pondered it in her mind. She regretted, when it was too late, that she had not allowed her prisoner to tell her more of his story.

CHAPTER VII

As the brother and sister walked home together Patrick said :

" Let's go to the studio for a bit. We don't want to hang about at home all day. Its so beastly dull at Craig Moor.

" But mother will be expecting you to lunch, Pat."

" Nonsense. She'll know that I'm staying with you at the studio. How stupid we were not to buy some food at Hartley, then we could have prepared it at your studio. Besides I want to see your new picture for the Academy. How are you progressing with it."

" My new picture is finished," said Elizabeth.

" Is it ? I suppose you, lucky girl, will send up more than one ? "

" No, I shall only send one this year—I haven't done much painting lately. I have been too busy over my fugues."

" For the life of me I can't understand how anyone wants to buy those fugues," said Patrick.

" Well, somebody does, and its a good thing for me, Pat."

"So it is, little sister, so it is." He suddenly linked his hand affectionately through her arm. "Listen, Betty, mine. We won't go to the studio to-day, but we'll take some lunch with us to-morrow and have a right good day there, and you shall play to me. I like your playing, I honestly do, and although I know nothing about music or painting, I admire your style. You are bold in your conceptions—you have a certain dash. You have a bold eye, little sis. You would never be a coward about anything."

"I hope not," replied Elizabeth.

"Well, now, I want to know if my dear little sister will help me a bit. Of course I am in money difficulties—I gave you to understand that last night, and also when I wrote to you."

"But why are you in money difficulties, Patrick?"

"Oh, for heaven's sake, don't begin to question. Think of the regiment I've been put into."

"You chose your own regiment."

"Stop that, I beseech of you. The thing to consider is this. I *am* in that regiment and I cannot live on my means in it."

"But wouldn't it be possible," said Elizabeth "for you to live on your means if you did *not* play bridge and billiards and put money on horses?"

"You seem to know a great deal about my life," said the young man.

"But, dear Patrick, it is true, isn't it?"

"It might be true or the reverse. The fact remains that I am short of funds—that I am heavily in debt—that unless I can gather, by hook or by crook, one thousand pounds by this day week, I shall be cashiered from the army."

The girl turned and faced him.

"You don't think a man will tamely submit to that sort of thing, do you?"

She continued to look him straight in the eyes.

"You owe one thousand pounds," she said in a low voice.

"Alas, I do."

"And who do you think is going to give it to you?"

"Well, Betty, you have been left two legacies."

"It is true that I've been left two legacies, which amounted altogether to one thousand pounds."

"Then there we are," said the young man, joyfully. "You will lend the money to me, your only brother. I don't for a moment ask you to give it. I can promise you six or even seven per cent. on it."

"But my dear Patrick, I haven't got a thousand pounds now."

"And why not? What have you been doing with your money? and in addition to your thousand pounds, you make, at least mother tells me so, largely on your pictures and music. I have no doubt that you have at the present moment to your credit at the very least fifteen hundred pounds, and yet you allow your only brother to go under. It comes to that, Betty, you allow it?"

His eyes, of the blackest brown imaginable, were fixed on her face. Notwithstanding all his efforts, they were cold, cruel, opaque eyes. They never could look soft like Elizabeth's glorious eyes. There was an absence of all soul in them. They were filled to the brim with self at its cruellest.

CHAPTER VIII

"Patrick," said his sister, "I must speak plainly and clearly—I have not got the money."

"And why may I ask have you not got the money—mother tells me you are simply rolling in money—with what you make by your pictures and that deadly stupid church music—as well as all the legacies that were left to you—? I fail to understand your remarks—unless indeed I understand them too well."

Here Patrick turned and stared at his sister —but on this occasion she kept her self-control and did not change colour.

"It is worse than absurd of you to talk as you do," continued the angry man, "No money indeed—what have you done with it?"

"It is absolutely unnecessary for me to tell you," replied his sister. My money that which I have earned and the little left to me in legacies belongs to me and I refuse to discuss the subject with you. Beyond the fact that I built the studio and paid most of the expenses of the organ, altho' father—dear man, did help me a little about the latter—I decline to be questioned—understand that Pat—I refuse to be questioned."

"Because you are afraid," answered Beaufort, in a low voice.

"You mistake—I am not in the least afraid—but to cut this unpleasant matter short—I will give you two hundred pounds—not a penny more."

Patrick was rather astonished by the firmness of his sister's voice. However, he was determined to come to close quarters with her.

"Elizabeth," he said, "You had best beware—two hundred pounds to a man who wants a thousand. The fact is I am not quite certain about your conduct of late and a desperate man will do desperate things."

"What do you mean?" she said, turning white.

"Ah, that's it, what do I mean? And what do *you* mean by changing colour. What did you mean yesterday by turning crimson when I spoke about the escaped convict. All the world knows that Adrian Trent is as good-looking a chap as ever breathed; even his convict clothes couldn't destroy his personal appearance."

"Patrick, I told you that I could and would help you to the amount of two hundred pounds.

But listen, I will not give you a half-penny, not a farthing if you say another word with regard to the escaped convict. I know nothing about the man and I refuse to be insulted by your remarks."

Patrick was rather astonished by the firmness of Elizabeth's voice; he changed his tune.

" All right, little sister, all right, but when a man is desperate and he is offered a quarter of a loaf."

" There is an old saying that half a loaf is better than no bread," replied Elizabeth, " and I presume you will take two hundred pounds from me, ill as I can afford to pay it. You certainly won't get any more."

" I'll have to speak to the gaffer, that's all," said Patrick. " Of course, there'll be an awful scene, but I must get through with it. I suppose you wouldn't speak to him for me, would you, Betty? He's awfully fond of you, you know."

Elizabeth considered for a minute. " I will if you like," she said. " I don't know that it will do any good."

They reached home. Immediately after lunch Professor Beaufort retired to his study; he was still fretting about the missing letters. He thanked Patrick for his cleverness in putting Mrs. Heavyfoot on the search for the Simpsons;

he said that Elizabeth had been very careless not to examine the pockets of the clothes she had given away. He looked with indignation at the daughter he really worshipped. But time was precious, he could not waste any more of it. He made his family a hasty good-bye, telling them not to disturb him even for a cup of tea in the afternoon, and went to his study. As soon as ever they were alone and Hephzibah had cleared away the luncheon things, Patrick turned to his mother.

"I have been talking to Betty, mother, she doesn't seem inclined to be generous."

"Oh, Betty! The poor fellow has been telling me, he really isn't to blame—it is some horrible bad young men who have come round him and who gave him false information with regard to horses—I really don't know anything about it, but I know Patrick is not to blame, and I know he has to find the money or he will have to leave the guards and what will your father say."

"Mother," said Elizabeth—she went up to the little woman and put her hand on her shoulder—"If I could save Patrick, I would, but honestly I have not got the money. I have at the present moment very little money, not anything like as much as you imagine. The little I have left I am desirous to keep,

MICROCOPY RESOLUTION TEST CHART

(ANSI and ISO TEST CHART No. 2)

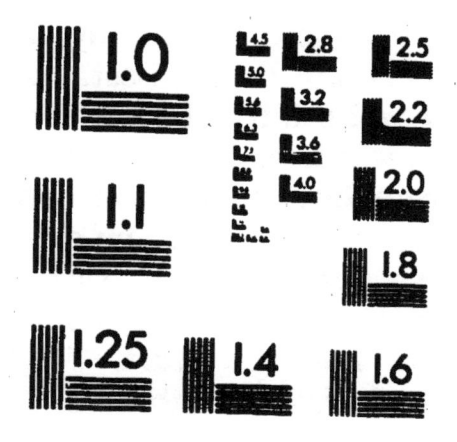

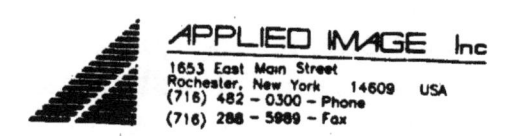

APPLIED IMAGE Inc
1653 East Main Street
Rochester, New York 14609 USA
(716) 482 - 0300 - Phone
(716) 288 - 5989 - Fax

but I told Patrick I would help him to the amount of two hundred pounds—more than that I will not give."

" There, mother, you hear her. A nice sister for an only brother to turn to."

" I do really think, Elizabeth, that you might help him a little more. Well, my darling, your mother at least will do her best. There is my jewellery—I will sell it. I have some valuable things and it will hurt me very much indeed to part with them, but you, my son, can take them up to London and get what you can for them."

" You are a dear," said Patrick. He stood over her in that half protecting, half petting way, which always won her heart. " There is no one like a mother," he continued, and then he stooped and kissed her very tenderly on her brow.

She looked up at him with adoration. Elizabeth felt a sick feeling going through her.

" Mother," she said, " I will speak fully and frankly and freely. You know perfectly well that this is not the first time that Patrick has come here for money. He will come again and again. Mother, you ought not to give away your jewellery. In a measure it belongs to me. I mean that it would be mine afterwards and I declare that you ought not to give it to him."

" You are a cruel girl," said Beaufort.

"I am not cruel, but I am just. Mother's jewels—I know exactly what she has got—will at the outside fetch one hundred and fifty pounds. You say you want a thousand pounds. Well, if I give you two hundred pounds and mother gives you, by depriving herself of all her little ornaments, one hundred and fifty more—that altogether amounts to three hundred and fifty pounds. How do you intend to make up the balance?"

"I thought the gaffer——"

"I know your father is worried by money on his own account just now," said Mrs. Beaufort. "Really, Betty, the whole thing turns on you. If you like, you can save your brother."

"I have given my ultimatum," returned Elizabeth. And then she turned to Patrick. "You have asked me," she said, "because you are too great a coward to do it yourself, to speak to father. Very well, I am going to him now."

She went proudly out of the room. Patrick watched her until she closed the door. Then he turned to his mother.

"I am very anxious about Elizabeth," he said.

"What do you mean, Pat?"

"Oh, nothing that I need trouble you about —but, let it be. If she thinks she can treat me as she is now doing, she will find that I have a handle over her which she will not like."

"I cannot imagine what you mean, my boy?"

"Mother, dearest, weren't you very frightened when that felon—that convict was abroad?"

"Oh, don't talk to me, Pat. What I endured there are no words to describe, and your dear father was so unreasonable. You know we had a fog, a dense fog, for over a fortnight, and the professor would keep the windows open even at night. I was nearly off my head with terror. Well, I must say Elizabeth acted splendidly then. However, the man escaped or died. There is no doubt on that subject now."

"None whatever, I should say," remarked Patrick, and he whistled very softly under his breath.

Suddenly the idea came to him that he would like to visit the studio alone without Betty, for Betty was so terribly alert and watchful. Before he brought any real pressure to bear on his sister, he must be certain of his convictions. He looked out of the window.

"Mother," he said, "do you mind if I take a walk?"

"Certainly not, my darling."

"Well, I have a fancy to go and see Betty's studio."

"Why go especially the '"

"I want to poke about and look at her pictures when she is not present. I am quite a fair judge of painting, although, of course, I know nothing technically about the art."

"Well, go if you like, dear. I am sure Elizabeth will not mind."

"I must have her key, though, mother, and to tell the truth, between you and me and the post, I would rather pay a visit to the studio on the sly. Just a bit of a lark, you understand. Then, to-morrow, when Betty and I go there I shall surprise her by my knowledge of her pictures. Can you manage to find the key for me, mother?"

Mrs. Beaufort said she would do her best. She searched and searched in vain for the key and as a matter of fact would not have found it, but just as she was leaving the room she trod upon something hard. It was the key of the old press where Elizabeth had hidden the convict's boots.

Mrs. Beaufort gave a little cry of pleasure when she found it, for she knew that her daughter kept her most treasured possessions in the old world press. How Elizabeth, so careful about most things, had managed to drop the key can never be explained, but dropped it she certainly had and Mrs. Beaufort now opened the press and soon found the key of the studio; she locked the press again and brought the press key down with her also to give to Elizabeth next time she saw her. She did not notice the large brown paper parcel. Had Patrick been with her his sharp eyes would certainly have lighted upon it.

"Here, Pat, here is the key of the studio, and don't be too long away, my precious boy. I see so little of you that every moment is of value to me."

"Oh, I'll be no time, mother. I'll just go and look round and come back primed with knowledge. It will be just a bit of a secret between you and me, but you may as well give me the key of the cupboard where Elizabeth keeps the studio key, then I can put it back again and she will never know."

"Well, I thought of putting it back myself. As a matter of fact I found the key in that old press Mrs. Tempest gave her when she left her the legacy."

"Mother, pray don't talk to me about that miserable legacy."

"Anyhow, Elizabeth is very proud of the old-fashioned press."

"All right, mother, I'm not going to run away with it. You may as well give me the key."

"I really think I would rather not, dear. I

will give it to Elizabeth and merely say I found it on the floor of her room."

" Mother, how disobliging you are. She will naturally wonder why you were in her room, then she will wonder why the key of her studio is missing, whereas if you give the two keys to me I can slip upstairs by and bye and put the studio key back and Betty will know nothing whatever of my interference."

As usual Patrick had his way. He went off whistling with the key of the press where Elizabeth kept the convict's boots reposing in his pocket.

Meanwhile Elizabeth, still holding her head very high and walking with the light, erect step, which always characterised her, reached the door of her father's study. She paused on the mat outside for a brief moment. She was anxious to calm the beating of her heart. She was so terribly angry, so deeply hurt, that at this moment it was possible for her to do something cruel towards Patrick. He, a man five years older than herself, to come down to their lonely home and demand all her little money— demand it, too, as a right. It was intolerable that anyone calling himself a man should act so. And finally he had deputed her to go between him and his father. Should she or should she not? Finally, she resolved to go through with it. She said to herself, "It doesn't matter." She was determined not to urge the question in any way. She would put the case before the professor and allow him to decide. He was no weakling like her poor, loving mother, he would be quite just, but he would be firm.

Elizabeth entered the room without knocking and stood before Professor Beaufort. The whole room was piled up with books, letters, papers. The professor's huge roll-topped desk was covered with letters and notes in his firm, strong, handwriting, scraps of manuscripts and proofs innumerable.

"Father," said Elizabeth.

He looked up, puzzled at the sound, then he passed his hand across his eyes and said,

"My dear, did I not tell you all that I was not to be disturbed until it was time to dress for dinner. Why this invasion of my priv:

"I was forced to come. I have son to say, which I think you ought to know

"Heavens!" sighed the professor, then he added the one word, "well?"

"It is about Patrick."

"I might have guessed it, Betty. That fellow, that waster, never comes here except when he wants money. Tell him at once and plainly that I haven't one penny to give him and go—go, Elizabeth. That is my answer. I have no money for Patrick, none!"

"Dear father, it is my duty to lay the case before you."

"Your duty, Elizabeth! Against my wishes!"

"Yes, it is my duty, for if nothing is done to prevent it, that may happen which will kill our mother."

The professor at these words seemed to wake up out of a sort of dream. He rubbed his hand impatiently again across his forehead, then he said:

"If it were Patrick I should take him by the shoulders and push him out of the room, but as it is you, Elizabeth, I respect your word. Now tell me what that waster—t.. : scoundrel has been doing."

"I don't know the full particulars," said Elizabeth. "I only know that he is heavily involved in debts of a nature which, if not met, will oblige him to leave the army."

"Well, let him leave the army."

"But, father, you don't quite understand. A young officer who expects promotion any day. Were he to leave the army now it would mean social and financial ruin. He would certainly have to fly the country, and mother—you know what she thinks of Patrick."

"I grieve to tell you, Elizabeth, that with all my love for her, I look upon your dear mother as a singularly weak woman—singularly, remarkably weak. Her son takes after her. Thank God I have a daughter with strength in her character. Well, what is the sum total. I always am tormented thus when I begin to see daylight."

"Father, it is a very large sum. He would not come to you himself so I volunteered to do so. I can give him two hundred pounds but not a penny more. Mother will help him by selling all her jewels which ought to bring in one hundred and fifty pounds. This makes a total of three hundred and fifty pounds."

"Then what on earth does the beggar want more? Three hundred and fifty pounds. I wish I could lay my hand on a sum like that."

"Unluckily he wants a thousand pounds."

"Let him go to—" cried the professor, and he used very strong language, not permissible to print.

Elizabeth sat very still without uttering a word. She knew quite well that her father would cool down after a time. She must wait until his wrath had abated. Presently he rose from his seat, knocking over a pile of books as he did so. Then he began to pace the room.

"Why had I a son born to me?" he murmured.

These words came to Elizabeth's ears as he slowly passed her.

"Why was a man child given to me?" was his next question. "Why are my grey hairs brought down in sorrow to the grave?" he said again. "Betty, you see before you a broken-hearted man. Betty, *you* ought to have been the boy—he'd have made a pretty girl, ha! ha! Dressed up, he would have made a good match with some fool—pity he wasn't the girl. You were meant to be the man. I'm proud of you, Betty—but that scoundrel! Do you mean honestly to tell me that he will take your mother's few jewels and two hundred pounds of your money."

"He will, father; He would take all my money if I would give it."

"You will not give it, will you, Elizabeth?"

"I have told him distinctly, father, that two hundred pounds is my maximum."

"Well, then, what have you come to me about?"

"I want to know if in any way you can—"

"I can—and I can't. You don't suppose I make much by this sort of work. I make, God knows, pleasure beyond words. I make delight unspeakable. I pry into the hidden mysteries, but money—cursed money—does not come much into this. No, Elizabeth, tell him that I've nothing for him. Tell him that

I wou'l not, if I could, and could not if I would. Do you suppose that I intend to leave your mother and you without bread to eat and clothes to wear and a home to shelter you. I am very far from rich but I am comfortably off unless he drains me as dry as he has drained every relation he knows. That is my answer. I have nothing for him, nothing at all, now go! Go, Elizabeth, go!"

"Father dear, I have done my best. Perhaps when you think things over you may just find it possible to add a little to the three hundred and fifty pounds, which mother and I can raise between us."

"I tell you, child, I haven't a penny; if I would, I couldn't—and if I could I wouldn't. Now, go!"

Elizabeth went. She felt sadder as she left the room than she had done yet. She entered the drawing-room. A fire burned in the grate—Hephzibah came in with the tea. Mrs. Beaufort was seated in her usual cosy chair—with her white Shetland shawl over her shoulders and her little, very precious, real lace cap on her head. She looked sweetly pretty, her dress was of black velvet—a treasure of bygone days—remodelled according to modern ideas. Her tiny hands were laden with rings of considerable value.

When Elizabeth entered the room she saw that her mother was looking at the rings and counting them.

"Well, Betty," she said eagerly, "what news?"

"Just what I expected, mother, father is adamant. He refuses to do anything."

"My poor boy," said Mrs. Beaufort.

"Mother, dear, do you think that Derrick is to be so dreadfully pitied? Of course I know that when we do wrong we are all to be pitied, but he did do wrong and that is an end of it. It is always unpleasant to have to pay the wages of sin, but they have to be paid."

"Oh, don't talk in that sanctimonious way, Elizabeth. Oh—oh—oh—do you think if I went to your father and fell on my knees and wept and wept—that he would relent? We could so easily draw some of our capital. I know for a fact that we have five thousand pounds in Consols. Surely we could manage with four thousand—and a thousand pounds would set the darling fellow up, and he has promised me so faithfully never as long as he lives to get into debt again. I am certain your father will yield when I speak to him."

"Mother, I should strongly advise you not to go to him. Patrick might perhaps speak. By the way, where is Patrick?"

Mrs. Beaufort smiled and looked knowing.

"He's out," she said.

"Out! what can he be doing?"

"Well, I wasn't to tell you—but I really don't see why you shouldn't know. He hasn't done anything dreadful, poor darling. He was so restless he felt he could not stay in the house. He was full of hope that you would succeed. He knows your great cleverness and power, but he said to me, 'I am too miserable to stay indoors,' so then it occurred to him that he would go to your studio and look at your pictures. Surely there could be nothing more innocent than that. And the joke is he does not want you to know he has been there, so you must keep it a profound secret."

Mrs. Beaufort was not glancing at Elizabeth. She was gazing into the glowing fire and sipping her tea and eating rich cake.

"You say that Patrick has gone to my studio, remarked Elizabeth. "But he couldn't do that for I have the key."

"Well, a funny thing happened," said Mrs. Beaufort. "Hand me that dish with the hot muffins, Elizabeth. Hephzie does them very well, doesn't she? I went to your room to look for the key. Of course I could not find it. You see you are so terribly neat. Any other person would leave the key on the dressing-table or the chest of drawers or the mantelpiece —a great strong key like that, but there wasn't a sign of it anywhere."

"Well, mother, go on." Elizabeth endeavoured to speak calmly.

"Just as I was leaving the room," Mrs. Beaufort continued, " such a funny thing happened. You dear little Betty, with all your thought and care, you are sometimes stupid. You know that old press Mrs. Tempest gave you ? "

Elizabeth was silent but her looks hung upon her mother's words.

"Personally," continued the mother, "I always thought that press was remarkably ugly, but Patrick says I have no taste, and that it would fetch a good sum at Christie's."

"It happens to be *my* press," said Elizabeth, "and I don't intend it to fetch a good price anywhere."

"You are so snappy, my darling, but mother does not mind. I found the key on the floor not far from your bed. I took it up, opened the press, and found, of course, on the second shelf the key of your studio. I locked the press again and gave the key to Patrick."

"Yes," said Elizabeth, "and what about—what about—" her voice shook in spite of herself. "What about the key of the press ? "

"Well, he insisted on my giving it to him. He said the joke would be to put the key back into the press and when you two went tomorrow to the studio, he would pretend that he knew nothing about the pictures. Now, remember, Betty, you mustn't betray me. I shouldn't have told you. It was very wrong of me to tell. Patrick will put the studio key back, and when he has done so, he will give me the key of the press."

Elizabeth sat mute like one stunned and dumb. She sat for a few minutes perfectly quiet.

"Why don't you take your tea? Have you nothing to say," remarked her mother.

"I don't want tea," she replied then. "I am going out to meet Patrick."

"You won't tell him what I said?"

CHAPTER IX

" You must leave all that to me, mother," said Elizabeth, endeavouring to speak as quietly as she could.

She ran swiftly upstairs. She put on her plain little hat and jacket. Whatever she wore she always looked like the perfect lady she was. She drew dark thick gloves over her capable but small hands. She locked the door of her room on the outside, slipped the key into her pocket, and went out to meet her brother.

Now there were two ways to the studio, one right over the hills. This was the shortest way. Another went round by the road. Elizabeth was puzzled as to which of these two paths Patrick would take. She thought, on the whole, he would go by the road as the safest and easiest, and return by the hills, for, coming back, it would be all down hill. She thought most anxiously, but did not think she had anything to fear by his poking and prying in the studio. She determined to meet her brother by the hill road. In a minute she was walking briskly. She was a splendid creature, so healthy, so well able to get out of every sort of difficulty, but now she was certain she was in the clutches of a wicked man, and that wicked man was her own brother. The only way to save herself and her people from dire disaster was to get the thousand pounds for Patrick. She thought of all possible means. She might sell out what was left of both her little legacies, but these had been terribly diminished by the expenses of the studio and the organ, and by the further expenses she had gone to for her prisoner, as she now invariably called Adrian Trent. There was a true man—a convict, but a *man*. It was worth spending money on him. How few were his words—how sombre his face, and yet how keen was the gratitude, and the *something else*, which she dared not think of, that shone out of his great sad eyes.

She walked up the hill and, as bad luck would have it, did take the wrong way.

Patrick went to the studio, took some time poking and prying, could find nothing to incriminate his young sister, and returned home as wise as he was when he left. He was cross, therefore, when he appeared again in the house. He pushed back the short curly hair from his forehead, and went into the little drawing-room.

"I say," he exclaimed, "how hot this room is! Mater, do you object to the windows being opened?"

"I have a cold, Patrick, but if you wish it——"

"Oh, a little fresh air will do no one any harm—I can't live in this atmosphere, and I am sure it is bad for you. Where on earth is Betty?"

"Patrick, you will be awfully angry with me, but I——"

"Yes, what have you done?"

"I told Betty about your going to the studio, and how I found the key of the old press."

"You told her! Really, mater, you are as weak as water."

"Oh, please don't scold me, Pat. The poor child was quite distressed, and I thought it would amuse and interest her—but——"

"Well, what did she do?"

"She was very angry when she found that you had carried off the keys of her old-fashioned press. She said she would go to meet you."

"I didn't see her. I suppose she took the hill road. Never mind, let's have a cup of tea."

Patrick drew forward the easiest chair in the room, sat back in it—crossed his legs—and allowed his mother to help him.

"Mother, this tea is overdrawn and quite cold. May I ring for some fresh?"

"Certainly, my darling."

Patrick got up lazily and rang the old-fashioned bell.

Hephzibah, as her manner was, poked in her head.

"Make some fresh tea with some boiling water," said the young officer.

Hephzibah promised to obey. "And bring some more bread and butter and hot muffins—I am starving. Whatever this air does—it is good for young appetites. Now, be quick, Hephzibah."

The girl moved very slowly and unwillingly.

When she had left the room, Patrick turned to his mother.

"I can't imagine why you and father, who are quite well off, should keep such a common-looking girl. She hasn't an idea how to behave. I couldn't bring a man from my company down here on any account whatever, with such a servant poking her head in and wearing her cap crooked. It is positively disgraceful. I often talk of my pretty mother and my handsome sister and my distinguished father, but I have to draw the line at any talk of coming to Craig Moor. I couldn't bring a fellow to dine, I really couldn't. You ought to have two servants at least."

"Hephzibah suits us perfectly, Patrick, and you give us so very little of your time, my boy.

I am sorry she displeases you, but I, myself, will wait on you as much as possible while you are here."

"Oh, thanks, mother, thanks."

Hephzibah returned with the freshly-made tea and provisions.

Patrick was just stirring his first cup when Elizabeth, heated from her rapid walk, came in.

"Patrick, where have you been?"

"Oh, mother let the cat out of the bag. I thought it would be such fun to pretend to know all about your pictures to-morrow, Betty. I had a daring little scheme in my head. I wanted to exclaim, when you showed me your big Academy picture, that it wasn't original, that I'd seen precisely the same picture in the studio of a friend of mine in St. John's Wood. Ha! ha! It would have taken a rise out of you, but the little mother cannot keep her dear little clapper quiet." Here he patted his mother's hand. She looked up at him with adoring eyes. "You saw the guv., didn't you?" he continued, and there was anxiety now in his voice.

"Don't mind about our father at present, Patrick. I want you to give me back immediately the key of my press."

"And what if I decline?"

"Then you don't get one perny of my two hundred pounds."

"Oh, is that the little game. Anyhow, we'll see."

"It is the truth, Patrick. I shall refuse to give you one penny unless you return me the keys of my press and my studio."

"Here's the key of the studio. I should like to examine that old press. I'm told it is a wonderful antique. You ought to sell it—you would get a great price for it."

"Sell Mrs. Tempest's present," said Elizabeth in a voice of scorn. "There's nothing whatever remarkable about it, Patrick, except that I want the key, and I *will* have it."

"No."

"Very well, you won't get a farthing from me. I was thinking that I might make my present to you—for to talk of it as a loan is absurd—two hundred and twenty-five pounds, but I must have the key."

"All right, if you are in the mind to help a chap, Betty, of course, I'm your slave. Here it is, and much good may it do you."

He dropped the key into his sister's hand. She put in into her pocket and then poured herself out a cup of tea, breathing a sigh of relief.

CHAPTER X

PATRICK BEAUFORT, who was the most observant of mortals, noticed his sister's sigh, and he was suddenly consumed with an intense desire to see the contents of the press. He kept that desire in the background at present, however. He settled himself, therefore, more comfortably in his easy chair, took no notice whatever with regard to Elizabeth's comforts, did not even get a chair for her, but said, in a voice into which intense excitement crept:

"Now, what about the gaffer? Good old gaffer—what will he stump up? I know he has, for mother told me, five thousand pounds put snugly away in Consols. He could easily sell out enough to make up my thou.—that is, with mater's jewels and your two hundred and twenty-five Here—I'll just jot down the amounts on a bit of paper."

He took an envelope and a gold pencil from his pocket.

"Mother's jewels will fetch one hundred and fifty—your little drop two hundred and twenty-five—that makes three hundred and seventy-five—balance six hundred and twenty-five. Surely there isn't a man in existence who wouldn't help his only son to the tune of that trifling sum."

"I'm sorry to tell you, Patrick, that father positively refuses to give you a farthing. You can speak to him yourself—I have paved the way for you. I have endeavoured to induce him to do something for you, but in vain. He says that if you do leave the army it will be a good thing."

"Oh, how awful," said Mrs. Beaufort. She shivered from head to foot. "Elizabeth, you absolutely speak in a cruel way. Pat, my darling, my own, we'll go at once to your father; he can't be unkind to you when I am by. He does love me—his little wife. I was always 'wee wifie' to him. I know he'll be good to you. Don't lose heart, my darling. We'll help you, my poor, poor boy."

"Well, let's go to him, mother, and get it done," said the young man roughly. "I must say, Elizabeth, you are a broken reed."

"I cannot agree with you," replied Elizabeth. "I mean to give you two hundred and twenty-five pounds. I do not consider that being a broken reed."

"What nonsense you talk, sis—when a man can't get free from his liabilities under a thousand pounds, what does two hundred and twenty-five pounds mean to him?"

"You can pay your creditors by instalments."

"Pay debts of honour by instalments!"

"Well, take the consequences. You knew quite well that we were poor, and you had no right to have debts of honour."

"There is no one in the world loves me except mother. I am certain she won't forsake me now."

"That I won't," said Mrs. Beaufort, "and while you have been out I have been examining my jewels, and I am quite sure they ought to fetch two hundred pounds. I shall miss my rings." She held out an exquisite little hand laden with jewels of many sorts and description. "But what are they compared to my boy," she continued. "Now, come, darling, we'll go and see father hand in hand—mother and son. He cannot reject our request."

The moment the pair had left the room, Elizabeth flew upstairs. What was to be done. She saw with those keen eyes of her's that Patrick suspected something. She guessed from the very first that Patrick had suspicions with regard to her. It was not merely for the sake of a practical joke that he had gone to her studio to-day. He had gone to pry and look

H

about him. Oh, how wise she had been to burn the convict's clothes the night before. But the boots—what was to be done with the boots? Whatever happened, she made up her mind to bury them that night, she must not hesitate—it was too dangerous. And yet the burying of a heavy pair of boots, with Patrick on the alert—Patrick desperately anxious on his own account, specially keen to get a handle over his sister, was a task of such immense difficulty, that she scarcely knew how she could accomplish it. She sat and wondered in her own mind which would be the safest course—whether it would be better to leave the boots where they were until he returned to London, which he would do very shortly, when he had got some money, even five hundred pounds, for he always grossly exaggerated his needs. But at the same time she doubted the expediency of leaving the boots where they might possibly be discovered at any moment.

She was standing in her room, looking from time to time at the reflection of her own young face in the tall glass which stood between the two windows when there came a tap at her door, and Hephzibah, according to her invariable custom, poked in her frowsy head and crooked cap.

"Miss Betty, it's you!"

"Yes, Hephzie, can I do anything for you?"

"There's a body of the name of Heavyfoot downstairs, who wants to have a talk, either with you or with Mr. Pat."

"Oh, I'll see her, Hephzie. Don't say a word to Mr. Patrick. I will come at once. Where have you put her?"

"I 'as her in the kitchen. She was that mortial tired from her long walk that I guv her a slice off the cold beef and a glass of beer. You don't mind, do you, Miss, darling?"

"Of course not, Hephzie, and the kitchen is as good a place as any. But I expect I must see her alone—can you manage to leave us for a short time."

"Is it me, missie—in course I can. I has a deal o' work in the scullery just now, and I'll lock the kitchen door, so that missus and that young gent can't get in if they was to try ever so. You run down and have your talk with her, Miss, dear. I must say you do look peaky. You've been doin' too much—workin' too much, I take it—but there, Miss Betty, you've Hephzibah on your side whoever goes against you."

In a very few minutes Elizabeth found herself in the kitchen. The kitchen was large and bright and clean, for Hephzibah, however untidy her cap and her hair, was an excellent servant. Elizabeth stood upright, facing Mrs. Heavyfoot. Heavyfoot both by name and nature, might this woman be considered. She had, however, a very keen and bright eye, and now her dark brown eyes, so common to the inhabitants of Hartleypool, were fixed with a certain anxiety on Elizabeth's young face. There was pity for Elizabeth, and at the same time a marked cupidity in her manner. She came up close to where the girl stood, and spoke in a thick muffled voice.

"I found this," she said, "and I thought ye'd best have it, having, so to speak, the best right to it. It's well young master didn't come acrost it—it's yorn at my price."

Elizabeth heartily wished that her colour did not change so perpetually. It was now an ashy white. She stretched out her hand, but the woman drew her's back.

"None o' that," she said. "Ye can't have it without a price—none o' that. I'm a pore woman."

Elizabeth's eyes grew round and larger than their wont. She had truly reason for her fears, for the woman had picked up a striped sock which belonged to a convict—a convict from Hartleypool prison, and she declared she had found it just outside Miss Beaufort's studio.

"I was walkin' there shortly after you and

young mister came yesterday, and I was turnin' and turnin' things over in my mind, and wonderin' what was to be done about the letters, and how I was to get them back for the professor, and to ask what I considered it was worth for the job. Although I may be a stout woman with little activity about me, owin' to a weight of flesh, I 'as a deal of activity in my mind. And there I seed lyin', just to the right, on a great blackberry briar—how it worn't seen long ago was a puzzle to me—but there it lay, within a stone's throw, a yard I may say, of your studio, Miss Beaufort—there lay the sock of the missing convict. Now, I says to myself, this is a bit of God's providence, and Miss Beaufort, for all her cares, is mixed up in it. I can take the sock straight to Captain Marshall, or I can give it to you. My price is ten pounds. You can take it, Miss, or leave it —it is nothing to me. It may lead to the discovery of Hadrian Trent, or it may do nothing. It's for you, Miss, to take it or leave it."

Elizabeth felt a queer kind of deadly sickness going over her. She knew that at any cost she must keep her self-control. She must not, on any account whatsoever, allow the woman to suppose that she was alarmed. At the same time, she felt herself in the dreadful position of one who must buy Mrs. Heavyfoot's silence.

She had, at that moment, no time to think coherently, or she would never have done what she did do. She looked into the low-class, crafty face.

"You want ten pounds for that sock," she said.

"And cheap at the price, Miss. You know, Miss Beaufort, that harbouring a felon means from two to four, or even five, years. Yes, Miss, that's what it means, for I axed my husband last night. I had the sock safe, and I didn't say a word to nobody, but I did say to Jim, 'What 'ud a body get that harboured that felon, Hadrian Trent?' 'Whym,' answers Jim, 'whoever the villain was who aided and abetted a felon and went agen the laws, he'd get his two, three, four or five year, accordin' to the circumstance. That's a positive fack,' says Jim, 'no doubt on the subject.' So then it come over me that I wouldn't like things to go hard on you, Miss—you were that good to my little Jennie when she had the scarlet fever, and the neighbours were afeard to come near the house. You brought her jellies and beef tea and tasty things, and helped me to get her into 'orspital, so I says to myself, I'll be good to Miss now."

Elizabeth thought very hard for a minute.

"I'll give you ten pounds," she says, "I do

not want that poor man to be caught. I do not acknowledge for a moment that I have anything whatever to do with his escape, but all the same, I would much rather he was not caught. Wouldn't you feel like that, Mrs. Heavyfoot? Think what a desperate fight he made for his liberty. Few men would have been so brave."

"Lawk a mercy," replied Mrs. Heavyfoot, "I don't agree with you one little bit, Miss. Fight for his liberty—why, he were a downright wicked man—a murderer, no less. Didn't he kill a poor young gel—didn't he stab her through the heart, and din't his own brother try for a time to save him by pertending to be the guilty party. Help to get a felon like that off—not me, Miss—not me."

"Well, I don't agree with you. I am by no means certain that the man was guilty, but, anyway, I am interested in those that are hunted—those who are down—those who are in trouble. That is my nature, and it will be my nature as long as I live. I will give you ten pounds, but how am I to ensure your silence."

"Ah, that's the question," said the woman. She had not thought of it until this moment, but now it loomed before her as a nice little nest-egg, for she could hold the striped sock over Elizabeth as long as Elizabeth was in the neighbourhood. She reflected on her own hard life and her husband's small wage—on her children's many requirements. She said to herself, "Here I be, and here's my chance."

"Well, Miss," she said, "ef you could give me ten pounds down and two pounds a month regular, you'd hear nothing more about the convict's sock until the trump of doom. There now, Miss, that's cheap, I take it, and I'm a Methody. I wouldn't break my solemn word for nobody."

Elizabeth looked distressed. She said:

"I will go up to my room and fetch you the money, and I will give you two pounds a month as long as you are silent."

Elizabeth flew to her room. She heard voices talking in the study, the angry voice of the professor, the pleading voice of her brother —the weeping voice of her mother. She was safe, so far.

She found that she had exactly ten pounds in her purse. She brought it down and put it into Mrs. Heavyfoot's hand.

"There," she said, "I want the convict to escape, so I give you the money. Where is the sock? I shall destroy it."

"And it is two pounds each month from now, Miss, as long as I keep the thing a secret."

"Yes." Elizabeth's voice was very low.

She felt a terrible sense of oppression. " Yes," she said, " two pounds a month. I will call at your house and bring it you. You'd better not be coming about here. It would only excite suspicion."

" I don't want you to be locked up, Miss."

" I thought you might like this jacket of mine thrown in," said Elizabeth. " It was left me by an old friend, and is a great deal too big for me. Now go, please. Remember, I trust you. Remember, that if you mention this matter to my brother, he has no money to pay you. He will promise you to any extent, but that is his way, but you'll never see the colour of his gold. Now, go ! "

" I'm arter thim letters," said the woman. " I allus likes to have a case on. Well, I'm about it now. Jim, he says, ' Maria, yer a born dertective. You'd catch 'em just like picking up pins,' he says, and it's true, for no one else saw that striped sock flung acrost the blackberry briar, but my sharp sight lighted on it fast enough.

Elizabeth said nothing further and the woman went away. Elizabeth went into the scullery. Hephzibah was there, looking flushed and excited.

" I do hope as that woman didn't want to injure you, missie."

"No, no, Hephzie, dear—no, no! It's—I think it's all right."

Then suddenly the girl flung her arm round the faithful woman's neck and burst into tears. They were the very first tears she had shed during all the awful weeks she had lived through. Her tears were violent and brief

"Hephzibah," she said, "I want a little fire in my bedroom to-night. It's laid, isn't it?"

"To be sure it is, Missie."

"Well, in that case, I shall put a match to it, for I feel rather chilly."

"No wonder, Missie, darling, spendin' so much time in your studio as you do, and you are always fretted to death when Mr. Patrick comes back. Ah, I 'as no likin' for him, and there's many moor girls can bear me testimony to the same. He's not a good man, is Mr. Patrick."

"I cannot talk of him now, Hephzibah, my heart is too sore. I will just light my fire and sit by it. You might bring me up a cup of tea by and bye, for I don't think I'll come downstairs again to-night. I have a racking headache."

Accordingly the girl went to her room, locked the door, lit the fire, and when it was burning brightly, she burnt the convict's sock. How it had got on the blackberry briar was a puzzle.

After it was consumed to ashes she regretted she had destroyed it. She began now to be certain that the whole thing was a smart move on the part of Mrs. Heavyfoot, that she had invented the whole story of the sock on the blackberry briar, for Elizabeth had felt certain on the previous night that she had burnt a pair of socks, not one.

"But I could not swear to it," thought the girl, "although certainly that was my impression."

Then it occurred to her how very easy it would be for Mrs. Heavyfoot to get a convict's sock through her husband. He often brought worn-out socks for her to darn. He was one of the officers at the prison, quite one of the low down officers, but still, he belonged to that dismal place, and his wife was paid a penny for every pair of socks she darned.

"What a fool I was," thought the girl. "If only I had looked carefully at the sock, I could quickly have dispersed her little game. Now I have, beyond doubt, given myself away. Oh, dear, what shall I do ? If that woman was meant to be a detective, I certainly was not."

Poor Elizabeth carefully pressed her hand against her violently throbbing heart, and said to herself :

"To be in the power of a woman like Mrs.

Heavyfoot! Well, at the worst she will keep silence for her own sake for a short time, and by then he will be safe, far, far away, quite out of reach. I suppose I could live even, even five years in prison!" A glow came into her cheeks and a bright light filled her eyes. " Yes I could do it—yes, joyfully, for my—my prisoner."

CHAPTER XI

In the course of that same evening there came a low and cautious tap at Elizabeth's door.

She got up from her small arm chair and unlocked it unwillingly—Patrick entered.

" Well sis," he exclaimed, " whatever is the matter with you ? "

" I have a bad head-ache," was the reply. All this horrible talk about money upsets me terribly."

" It cannot upset you more than it upsets me, poor little girl. The gaffer has sprung fifty pounds just to please the mater—mean I call it—don't you ? "

" No, Patrick, I think it was very generous of my dear father."

" Oh ! I might have guessed you would take his part—I and the mater—you and the pater—so gags the world. I can tell you I had a rare tustle even to get that beggarly drop, still I have now secured over four hundred and twenty five pounds—not half what I want—but better than nothing. I can, at least, get rid of my most alarming debts of honour now and can go on for a bit. I shall leave here at an early hour to-morrow morning."

The girl felt a sudden sense of untold relief—Patrick watched her narrowly out of his keen and yet opaque eyes. His eyes were large and very black, they were at once extremely watchful and at the same time destitute of all soul. They were more the eyes of an animal. than those of a man.

"If I were you, Betty, I'd go to bed," he said.

"I will take the hint, Pat, after you have left me."

"How is it, Betty, that you and I are never good friends?"

The girl gave him a keen, long look.

"Because we are as the poles asunder;"

"That's true enough," he answered, "but why are we as the poles asunder? We were born of the same parents. Why should you think in one way and I in another?"

"Oh, Pat, if you were different, how I should love you," said the girl, her beautiful eyes kindling and the colour rushing into her cheeks.

"And if you were different, how I should love you," was his reply. "If you were like an ordinary sister, you would help a chap in his trouble. Well, I have come now to say that I'm leaving here and may not return for a very long time. I shall try to effect an exchange into a foreign regiment and, believe me, that exchange will not come to pass for nothing. But now, listen, Betty, I want to say something."

"If it is anything unpleasant don't say it. I have a dreadful headache and can't stand unpleasant subjects."

"You shrink away from what you call unpleasant subjects, just like a girl whose heart was broken. You are not a bit like the old Elizabeth. Don't you remember the time when I brought young Franks down—didn't we have a gay time then?"

"I don't remember," said Elizabeth, "was it a long time ago?"

"There you are, you take no interest in anything. I will tell you why you are changed. You've had dealings with that chap, Adrian Trent, and if I weren't the decent fellow I am, I should make up the odd money I want by going to Captain Marshall and putting the law upon you and upon him."

"Patrick, if you really believed what you say, you could not get your own sister into disgrace. Besides, I have nothing to do with the escaped convict."

"I say, my dear, you have. Nothing could have been easier for you than to hide that abandoned wretch in your studio. It was a nice thing for my sister to do, and I don't believe you can deny it."

Elizabeth suddenly sprang to her feet.

"Suppose," she said, "just for the sake of supposing that what you imagine is the case, would you, your own sister's brother, subject her to imprisonment—to disgrace—to a public trial? Would you indeed do that, Patrick—do you think it would look well in the eyes of the world?"

"No, I don't think it would look well."

"Then, of course, even though you have your suspicions, you must keep them to yourself, for you cannot by any possibility betray your own sister—even granted that I am the guilty wretch you consider me."

"I thought I'd mention it," said Patrick. "Don't fidget, little sister, if ever you get into trouble it won't be through Patrick Beaufort. And now good-night. I'm off at a very early hour in the morning. By the by you will give me that cheque, won't you?"

The girl went wearily to her desk. She opened it, took out her cheque book and wrote a cheque for two hundred and twenty-five pounds.

"Its a miserable pittance," said the young man.

"Well, Pat, don't take it, because it is anything but a miserable pittance to me. It means hours and days of toil. I don't like my money to be called a miserable pittance—it is a very great deal for a sister to give a brother, and a brother ought to be bitterly ashamed to take it."

"Oh, that sort of thing is left out in me," said Patrick. "I don't mind a bit taking mother's jewels. Poor dear little mums, she has stripped herself bare. She almost offered to give me her wedding ring, but I did draw the line at that. I have feeling in me somewhere. As to the governor, he gave his wretched pittance of fifty pounds with such a snarl and such a look at my face that I felt the sooner I left him the better. He has, at any rate, made the matter a necessity. Now I think that's about all. When you hear from me next little sister, I shall probably be preparing for a sojourn in the east. Meanwhile, you keep clear of convicts. Ta-ta, my love, ta-ta."

So Patrick went away, leaving Elizabeth standing numb and cold, notwithstanding her fire, in the centre of her little room. She could not bury the boots that night, and yet the boots must be buried. She had little fear now with regard to Adrian Trent. He was on board the

Lusitania by now and he was the sort of man who would do well in another country. Nevertheless, she was anxious to keep all suspicions at bay until after the *Lusitania* reached New York and Henry Councellor had started on his new life. After that, nothing could injure him.

Elizabeth was not a girl to fall in love easily. There was something very reticent and reserved about her nature. Her soul dwelt in deep places where it could not be got at except under exceptional circumstances. Why, Elizabeth Beaufort, coming of a noble race, highly educated, well bred in every sense of the word, should have given her heart to a man who had escaped from prison, was a marvel which could scarcely be accounted for, yet such was the case. The man was innocent and a gentleman, as she expressed it over and over again. He dwelt in her heart. She would never allow him to tell her what he had done. She never expected to see him again. She knew that such a meeting would be most fatal for her, but she also knew that no other man could take his place in her soul. She believed absolutely in his innocence, she believed in the noble expression of his face. Had he been a guilty convict she would have helped him, but being what she knew he was, it was her delight to go through peril for his sake. She wished she had the gift of second sight and could see him now. Was he thinking at all about her—was he remembering those days when he sat with the windows closed and the curtains drawn listening to her music. Did he recall the time when he said, " I am accused of bloodshed "—nevertheless, knowing this fact, she still held out her hand for his clasp, and then he had fallen on his knees and kissed it. Ah, yes, their two souls were one.

" But I will not mind five years in prison for his sake," thought Elizabeth, " if it comes—if it comes."

Her last waking thought was the certainty that it would come, that beyond doubt Mrs. Heavyfoot would betray her. Mrs. Heavyfoot had already secured ten pounds. This fact was so black against Elizabeth that scarcely anything further was necessary. She had but to go to the governor and claim at least a part of the reward for the capture of Adrian Trent. Elizabeth could only hope that the woman would do nothing until he was safe under his new name at the other side of the world. It was highly probable that she would do nothing for a few months at least.

Meanwhile Mrs. Heavyfoot went back to her house in the town of Hartley. It was a good sized house and by no means clean. Mrs.

Heavyfoot was a very untidy woman. Her husband had just come in. He was washing his hands at the sink.

"Supper ready, old gel?" he called out.

"Not yet, Jim—I've been away—I've been busy."

"I wish to goodness, Maria, you would have supper ready when I come in. I got to go back to the prison immediately arter. Ef I don't attend to my duties I'll never get into the second rank of officers and I want to get into the first rank."

"All in good time," said Mrs. Heavyfoot.

She pounced across her untidy little room. She took off her small, ill-fitting bonnet—she smoothed back her rough black hair. The children came in hungry—ravenous for their food. She told them to get out of her sight. They fled. They knew that mother had a heavy hand as well as a heavy foot. They disappeared and began their play—the invariable play of such children in the little street outside.

Heavyfoot sat down in the only easy chair and looked with gloom in his eyes at his uncomely wife.

"I can't think, for the life of me, why ye don't act like Mrs. Price and Mrs. Jennifer, Maria, but you are always behind time."

"Behind time be I? You talk, Jim, about what yer know and when yer don't know anythink keep silence. That's all I got to say."

"You're in a rare bit of a temper, old woman. I want my supper, and if I can't get it, I'll go without it."

"Well, do give a body a minute's peace. I can't cook in no time, can I? I've got a lovely bit of liver, calves' liver, too, and bacon and cold taters for supper, and I'll have them all frizzling in a jiff."

As the woman spoke she put a frying-pan on the fire, and soon the bacon, liver and taters were frizzling in a very agreeable way. The man sniffed at the savoury smell. The children came and peeped in at the window.

"There's such a lot of them," said Mrs. Heavyfoot. "I wish to goodness I hadn't such a big family."

"You have the childher God Almighty sent you, Maria, and you ought to be proud of 'em."

"Wull, I aint that's flat. I'm tired to death. Its work, work from mornin' to night. If only I had the luck to be young miss yonder."

"What young miss?"

"The only young miss in these parts—Miss Elizabeth Beaufort. If I was her, living at her ease with that good-for-nothing Hephzibah to wait on her, and her mother and her father petting her like anything, and a grand bedroom all to herself and she with what they calls a stoodio—a mighty convanient thing a stoodio can be at times!"

The woman looked knowing, but Heavyfoot was too anxious for his supper and too keen to get back to his duties to comment just then on his wife's words. When the fry was brought to perfection the table was laid with a cloth by no means clean, on which was placed knives and forks, which badly required the attention of a good, capable housewife.

Billy, the eldest boy, was then sent to a public house for a jug of beer. He came back with it brimming over and said:

"Mother, mother—"

"Set down and stop talkin', Billy."

"Mother, they do say as mayhap they'll light upon that Hadrian Trent after all."

"Don't ye listen to silly gossip," said Mrs. Heavyfoot, who for reasons of her own did not wish anyone to be in at the capture but herself.

Heavyfoot pricked up his ears, however.

"Draw your chair into the table, my boy. Come, children—I'll give ye a drop of beer each if ye are good. Now then, mother, draw in."

"I'm sure I'm hungry enough," said Mrs. Heavyfoot, "haven't I been tramping it all day. I hope you are prepared to give me an extra pair of boots, Heavyfoot."

"An extra pair of boots—why, I guv ye a pair not a month back."

"Wull, I'll ask for 'em when I want 'em. Maybe, I can manage for myself. I 'as my own little store, ha—ha!"

Here she laughed in a boisterous manner. Her children all looked at her in alarm. Lizzie, the youngest of the group nestled up to her father's side. She was his pet—his darling. He put his strong arm round her and presently took her on his knee.

"Does Lizzie like liver and bacon," he asked.

"'Ees, veddy much," said the small child.

"Don't you give her much, Jim," shouted Mrs. Heavyfoot, "her'll have howling croup or somethin' of that sort in the dead of night and you away—and I can't be disturbed. A woman as tramps can't be disturbed."

"What in the world are ye tramping about, may I ax?" inquired her husband.

"Have ye sense at all in your head, Jim? Didn't I tell ye that young miss and master—he's an elegant man is young master—come down here looking for them Simpsons. It seems this way. Miss, who takes all the wicked part of the population on her shoulders—mark my words, Jim—all the wicked part of the population—some lydies are made like that. She guv a whole packet of letters cf her father's in a coat to that man Simpson, and natural-like, the poor professor wanted his letters back. And miss, she come to ask for them, and Mr. Pat, he looked werry knowing—I will say that for him, werry knowing—and he says to me, says he, " Them letters must be found," but miss—she didn't seem to care a bit. She said, ' as the Simpsons have gone, it can't be helped,' but the young master he says, ' Find them letters,' he says, and he places his hand, gentleman-like, on my shoulder. He says, ' Mrs. Heavyfoot, you find them letters,' and he looked at me so earnest, and I says to myself, 'There's money in them letters—I'll find 'em.' "

" You are a rare 'un for money," remarked her husband, as he helped himself to a fresh bit of bacon.

" Yes, and by all token, I'm a good one for cooking a bit o' liver and bacon," said his wife.

Later on that same evening, when all the children had gone to bed, and the husband's last duties at the prison were over, and he had unexpectedly come home, he found, somewhat to his amazement, his wife, Maria Heavyfoot, sitting up waiting for him. He was by no means gratified at seeing her, for he had a private store of whiskey, which he indulged in when he had a chance like the present. He kept it in a cupboard where his old boots and other old things were piled. He usually took a swig from the bottle before he went to bed, but he could not do so now with Mrs. Heavyfoot's large, crafty face gazing at him.

"Why, in the name of thunder, are you up, Maria?" was his remark.

"Because I been puzzling something out in my 'ed, if you must know."

"Puzzling out something in your head?"

"That's about it, old man."

"Well, whatever is it, old gel? I must go to bed or I'll catch it in the morning. There's a rum lot expected to-morrow—Hadrian Trent ain't nothing to 'em. They say they are a whole band of gentleman burglars, and they are to be treated mighty sharp—no difference made between them and the roughest of the rough. That's fair, say I."

"And so say I," replied Mrs. Heavyfoot. "Why ever should we have pampered gentlefolk when they stoops to crime. Why should us do it?"

"Well, we don't do it, so you needn't think on the subject," said Heavyfoot. "And now you'll be off to bed, for its mighty late."

"I will, after I've had my bit of a say. I wants to know what sort o' reward will be guv to the one as lays a finger on Adrian Trent?"

"What reward—the reward ain't mentioned, but reward there'll certainly be."

"How much do ye think?"

"Well, I shouldn't be surprised ef the government rose as high as seventy-five pounds. I've no right to say it for it ain't in my department," here the man laughed, "but I shouldn't be surprised."

"Seventy-five pounds," murmured Mrs. Heavyfoot. What was two pounds a month compared to seventy-five pounds.

"And ef, supposin'," she continued, "a person—I'm not sayin' who and I'm not sayin' anybody, but supposing a body put evidence in the way of the governor what 'ud lead to the discovery of Hadrian Trent without gettin' him sharp on the nail, would that person get a reward?"

"I've no doubt of it, in fact I'm sure of it. But I wish I could see what was in the back o' your nut, old woman. Whatever are you thinkin' of?"

"Nothing, Jim, nothing at all. I've only just had a thinking fit on. Them Simpsons going off with the letters. I'm determined to get them letters."

"Well, get them woman, but for heaven's sake get to bed."

The man spoke in a gruff voice. He drew himself up to his full height. He was a powerful fellow, as he had need to be in his special calling. Mrs. Heavyfoot looked at him with pride.

"It'd be good for your credit if that Hadrian Trent was caught, wouldn't it?"

"How you do hark back to that man, woman," said Heavyfoot. "You've got something in your nut, not a doubt of that."

"Wull, and ef I have—I'm not going to show it to you. Ef I can catch Hadrian Trent, maybe I will and maybe I won't. It all depends."

CHAPTER XII

EARLY the next morning Patrick Beaufort bade his sister an affectionate good-bye. He bestowed a stiff one on his father, and one full of love on his mother. He let her cling to him and pressed her very close to his heart.

" There's no one like a mother," he repeated in his rich, seductive voice.

She laid her head on his breast and shed bitter tears.

" Oh, my own, own boy," she said, and then she inserted a ten-pound note, which she had been saving for a birthday present for Elizabeth, into his palm.

That palm closed greedily over it. When did it ever refuse to close over any sort of money!

A cab had come from Hartley for the young man. He was far too grand to walk the distance, although for the visit to his parents he had only brought a suit case.

Elizabeth felt a great sense of relief at his departure and, determined that come what might, she would bury the boots that night.

It was not a specially good night for the purpose, for the moon was almost at the full, but she felt the danger of delay. She had a curious sensation, too, of being watched. This was doubtless caused by Mrs. Heavyfoot. To be in the power of Mrs. Heavyfoot was torture to the proud girl. Nevertheless, it was scarcely likely that Mrs. Heavyfoot would wander the moors at the time when Elizabeth buried the convict's boots.

The moon was now nearly quite at the full, and it shed a pale radiance on the quiet face and stately figure of the young girl, as she set out on her self-appointed task about one in the morning. With the boots carefully wrapped in the same paper in which she had folded them when taking them from the studio, the girl placed them under her arm, slipped out of the house, went to the back premises, and secured a spade and trowel, and thus equipped, started on her journey into the neighbouring woods. There was a fringe of forest trees about half-a-mile away. Elizabeth sooned reached this fringe. All was perfectly still, but the girl could not help starting once or twice, so like were some of the reflections of the bare branches of the trees to human figures, to monsters with huge, unwieldy hands, to giants with outspread arms, to everything that was grotesque and horrible.

She chose a spot which was very secluded. She had already made up her mind to bury one boot in one place, and one in another. That would certainly double her labour, but it would make the concealment safer. She accordingly dug a deep hole with her spade, shovelled out the earth with her trowel and laid a boot within. As she did so, she knew well that she was trembling. He had worn it when he escaped—it was on his foot during those awful days of hunger and terror. She pressed it now into mother earth.

"Keep it, mother earth," whispered the girl, under her breath. "Be good, keep it safely until the Last Trump."

Then she shovelled back the loosened earth and pressed the leaf mould over it, and made the place look exactly as though it had not been disturbed.

She wandered a little further into the wood and found a suitable place for the remaining boot; this also she buried in safety. She then returned home. She did not meet a soul, either going or coming. She knew that she would incur great danger if she did, for anyone who had seen her carrying a spade and trowel must, to say the least of it, have wondered at her possible errand.

Elizabeth now got safely into the house,

first of all putting the spade and trowel into their usual place in the out-house. Their faithful old dog growled slightly, but at a word from his beloved mistress, he wagged his tail. A few minutes later the tired, but now happy, girl was fast asleep. Little did Elizabeth guess, little did she know, that step by step, a shadow had really followed her, always keeping well within the shade, always remaining in the blackest part of the forest, but witnessing all— witnessing the burying of the first boot and the second boot. It did not matter in the least to Mrs. Heavyfoot, when she had accomplished her task, *how* Elizabeth got home. She knew that the wide expanse of moonlight made it impossible for her to hide from the girl, but in the forest she was safe enough.

Mrs. Heavyfoot felt restless, wild to get the reward, which was still offered for the missing convict. Mrs. Heavyfoot could scarcely rest in her excitement. She crept noiselessly into her little house. She did not dare to go upstairs to wake Jim. Jim was again sleeping at home. She crept slowly into a room on the ground floor and lay down beside her little girl. The child was glad enough to snuggle to her mother, who, as a rule, was rough and cross to her. Mrs. Heavyfoot was thinking of all the golden things in store, the certain promotion for Heavyfoot, the large sum of money which would be put into her hands. She would take good care of that. She thought of her neighbours, Mrs. Jennifer and Mrs. Price, who were often brought up to her. Soon she would have a superior house to theirs. She would be, in fact, *the* woman of the colony. Yes, she had now the whole thing at her fingers' ends. The burying of the boots made assurance doubly sure.

On the following morning, a lovely day, when Elizabeth sang over her work, Mrs. Heavyfoot, for a very different reason, felt inclined to sing over her's. She was determined to keep her information entirely to herself, but she had laid her plans.

CHAPTER XIII

EARLY the next morning the children were packed off to school. They had enjoyed quite a fair breakfast for children in the Heavyfoot class, and they carried in their school bags their meagre lunch, consisting of a hunch of bread each, and a lump of very strong—common cheese. The bigger children had more in quantity in the way of food than the younger ones, but their mother, as she saw them on their way, gave them all clearly to understand that they would not be welcomed home until time for father's supper, when, if they were all good, they might each have a sip out of father's jug of beer. Then Mrs. Heavyfoot turned her attention to Lizzie—Lizzie was the youngest of the family, her father's pet, and too young for school—for there was no kindergarten in the neighbourhood. Now, as Mrs. Heavyfoot meant to be out all day she did not want to be bothered—as she expressed it—with Lizzie. She accordingly carried the child across the road to Mrs. Jennifer. She despised Mrs. Jennifer very heartily in the night watches, but she found this bright, most good-humoured young woman more than useful when she wished to go out.

"Wull ye tak care of Lizzie for me?" she called out as she entered uninvited the spotless home of the Jennifers.

Mrs. Jennifer's kindly face beamed all over.

"To be sure I will so," she remarked.

"I'll be greatly obliged, and when my ship comes in I won't forget it of you. I'm after them stupid letters, they're worritting of me."

"What letters?" asked Mrs. Jennifer.

"Haven't you heard? Well, to think of that. You remember them Simpsons?"

"I do," said Mrs. Jennifer. "To tell the truth, I pitied them dreadfully. I can't imagine why ever they come *here* to live. I suppose that miserable man Simpson thought he'd get taken on at the prison, but he wasn't the kind. The governor would have nothing to do with him."

"Well, be he what he were," said Mrs. Heavyfoot, "I had no fancy for him, and, as a matter of fact, he decamped without paying his rent. But you are one of the softies, ain't you, who *pities* wrong-doers? I'm not made that way, and I thank God Almighty for it every day on my bended knees."

"Then, surely, you might thank God Almighty for something better." Mrs. Jennifer put little Lizzie, as she spoke, into a small chair, which her own dead baby had used, and gave her some of the dead baby's toys to play with.

" 'Ook, mummy, 'ook," said the little one, raising rapturous eyes to her mother's hard face.

" Well, I'm arter them letters," said Mrs. Heavyfoot, not taking the least notice of her child. " You see, it were like this. Miss, she come along—— "

" You mean Miss Beaufort ? "

" I calls her ' miss '—she comes along, jest as she allus do—a more prying young woman I never come across—— "

" A more beautiful young lady, more like an angel *I* never come across," said Mrs. Jennifer, " and you're cruel hard to speak as you do of her ; I've a good mind to send Lizzie back with you."

On hearing these words Lizzie set up a howl.

" No, no, my pretty one, I'll keep you fast enough," continued the young woman, bending down over the child and kissing her.

" Wull," said Mrs. Heavyfoot, " we each has our opinions of our neighbours. We'll each wait and prove *who's* right in this matter. I says miss is a prying sort."

" And yet she nursed your child through scarlet fever when no one else would come near you, and she give you strong beef tea, and eggs and cakes and jellies. I wouldn't speak of one who was kind to me like that—I."

" Well, leave her alone," interrupted Mrs. Heavyfoot, " I've no time to waste. I'm going to find Simpson, if he's alive."

" Whyever don't ye leave the poor man alone, he don't owe *you* no rent ? "

Mrs. Heavyfoot heaved a deep but triumphant sigh.

" He owes me summat better than rent," she remarked, "but there, I can't waste my time no longer. So long—till I come again for Lizzie."

Mrs. Heavyfoot left the cottage. Her first act was deliberately to call at the prison. She asked to see Captain Marshall. She told the warder that she had " summat of importance to say to his highness."

In a very short time she was conducted to the room in which the governor waited for her. Captain Marshall knew the wives of all of his staff very well, and Mrs. Heavyfoot had the sort of face and figure which could not be easily forgotten. It was so hard, so stout, so cruel.

" Sir, your highness— " she dropped a profound curtsey, " I wants to ax ye a question."

" If you have only to ask me a question, I'm afraid I shall have to tell you to go," said

Captain Marshall. "I'm far too busy to answer questions."

"I suppose, captain, all the same, that ye want to get back that villain, Hadrian Trent."

"What, have you news of him?" said the captain, his manner changing.

"I don't say yes, and I don't say no. What I want to know is this. Supposin' I was to tell you things that 'ud lead to his capture, the scoundrel—what sum in money 'ud you give me. I don't suppose you'd take a pore woman's time and knowledge for nothing."

"I would give you," said Captain Marshall, "if, eventually, the information you choose to impart to me led to the re-capture of Trent, the sum of twenty-five pounds."

This was not at all what Mrs. Heavyfoot expected.

"That's all," continued Captain Marshall, "have you anything more to say?"

"I have, captain—your highness—but I must consider first how much your offering is worth."

"I will wish you good-morning, Mrs. Heavyfoot, and don't come to me again until you are prepared to *say* something, for I have no time to waste on idle gossip."

"What a great chump of a fellow he be," thought Mrs. Heavyfoot, as she wended her way in the direction of Craig Moor, "but I'll have the right side of him yet, see if I don't."

She laughed several times as she walked. Her laugh was harsh and cruel, it was the sort of laughter which a satyr might have. Once she stood still and stamped her foot. She was standing then very near Elizabeth's studio.

"Ah, I did it fine," she said to herself, "I did it cunning. Nobody knows that I tuk an old sock as belonged to another feller, and pertended to my husband that it got burnt, and stuck it on the blackberry briar. Nobody knows that, but all the same it'll do for miss. I ain't calling her Miss Elizabeth or Miss Beaufort. She's miss to me, and she'll be in gaol soon, or my name ain't Heavyfoot."

The woman walked on again. As she reached Craig Moor, she suddenly encountered Elizabeth Beaufort.

"How do you do, Mrs. Heavyfoot," said Elizabeth.

The woman gave an awkward bob. She looked full into the eyes of the girl.

"I wants your 'pinion of twenty-five punds?"

"I am in a great hurry," replied Elizabeth, "I have no opinion to give you. It would be a large sum for you, a comparatively small sum for me, that is all I can say."

"Oh, ye're off to yer *stoodio*. It's a werry conwenient place, that stoodio—it's a place what 'as its uses. They say there's music made there and paintings made there—and—we won't talk of what else is made there. We won't talk of the hidden things that are put away there—no, we won't—that we won't."

"Mrs. Heavyfoot, I have no time to talk to you now. Good-morning."

Elizabeth passed out of the gate as the woman passed in. Mrs. Heavyfoot turned and glanced after her. She noticed her beautifully-formed, erect young figure, her fine swinging walk. She noticed all these things without noticing them. To her it was nothing that Elizabeth Beaufort was beautiful. She knew her to be an accomplice in the escape of a felon, and she was thinking how much twenty-five pounds was worth. She'd got ten pounds already from Elizabeth, and she was promised two pounds a month beside. That would make twenty-four pounds a year. Twenty-four pounds a year would mean, at the end of two years, forty-eight pounds. Surely that was more than twenty-five pounds. Was it worth her while "to run her in," as she expressed it.

After a little time of reflection, however, she determined to go round by the kitchen entrance and tap at the kitchen door. Hephzibah had no love for the woman—she knew that she was spiteful—she knew also that Mrs. Heavyfoot was anxious to get her daughter Juliana into Hephzibah's place at Craig Moor. She was, therefore, very chuff in her manner. She did not even ask Mrs. Heavyfoot to come in. She stared at the woman, and the woman stared at her.

"Wull," she said, "ain't you going to give a body so much as a set-down, after coming all the way from Hartley?"

"You're welcome to come in," said Hephzibah, "ef you'll only stay a minute or two. My master and my mistress wouldn't send a beggar from their door."

"A beggar indeed," said Mrs. Heavyfoot.

"Wull, you seem mighty like one; anyhow, I've seen beggars a sight better than you."

Mrs. Heavyfoot snorted, but she had her work to do, and must, if possible, remain civil. She entered the kitchen, sank into a chair, and said, in a low voice:

"I 'as a great drought on me."

"Has ye," replied Hephzibah.

"Yus, I say it, it's true."

"Wull, there's water from the pump. Ye can have a glass ef ye have a likin' for it."

Mrs. Heavyfoot sat still for a minute, then she said slowly:

"I could do with a glass of stout or a glass of beer. It seems shameful like for rich folks like them Beauforts to give a body only a glass of water—and I could do for 'em. You don't know what handles I 'as over them—and over miss in especial."

Hephzibah turned very white. Her inclination was to take the heavy woman and push her out of the door. She decided, however, for Elizabeth's sake, to be civil. She said, after a pause:

"I can't give what don't belong to me, but I'll ask my mistress, and I've no doubt she'll let me draw half-a-pint for ye."

"There now, that's more tidy-like," said Mrs. Heavyfoot.

Hephzibah went into the dainty little drawing-room where Mrs. Beaufort spent most of her time.

"Ma'am," said Hephzibah, "there's one of thim officer's wives 'as called here."

"Oh, what about?" said Mrs. Beaufort.

"Well, ma'am, she says she's mighty thirsty and she axes for a glass of beer."

"Certainly, Hephzibah, give her a glass of beer and a slice of the kitchen cake."

"It's too good for her, ma'am, I don't like her."

"Why, who is she?" asked Mrs. Beaufort, looking up with sudden interest.

"Heavyfoot, by name," said Hephzibah.

"Heavyfoot," repeated Mrs. Beaufort, "I heard my dear son speak of her. I may come into the kitchen by and bye to see her. Mr. Patrick said she was a clever, discerning sort of woman."

"Oh, she be all that, ma'am, but if I was you I shouldn't trouble to put my foot inside the kitchen while she's there."

"I shall please myself about that, Hephzibah. Go and give the poor woman her beer. If she has walked all the way from Hartley she must be very thirsty."

Hephzibah returned to the kitchen. She drew a small glass of beer. Mrs. Heavyfoot remarked on the size, but the cut from the kitchen cake mollified her. Meanwhile Mrs. Beaufort, having thought and thought finally became restless, rose to her feet, sat down again. At last, with a faltering step, for she was a very frail little woman, she left the drawing-room and went along the passage. She opened the kitchen door, making an excuse on her way.

"Hephzibah," she said, "Oh—I didn't know you had a visitor—Hephzibah, I was thinking that we would have a boiled apple pudding to-night. How do you do, my good woman, I don't know your face."

Mrs. Heavyfoot had finished her beer and every crumb of her cake.

"Apple pudding for the rich," she said, "I wish my poor Lizzie had a bit of apple pudding—it be rare and tasty, that it be."

"What's your name, my good woman," said Mrs. Beaufort.

"Heavyfoot," was the reply.

"Oh, then, I know about you. My son has told me about you."

"Eh now, 'ave 'ee, and ain't 'e a 'andsome gent—I never see 'is like. Why, my heart it just pops up and down when I see him—he's a beautiful gent and as good as he's beautiful. You must be proud, ma'am, to have a son like that."

"I am," said Mrs. Beaufort, much interested.

"Well, ma'am, I've called to tell Hephzibah—I little thought to have the great honour of speaking to your leddyship—I've called to say that I'm on the search for thim Simpsons."

"Yes?" said Mrs. Beaufort.

"I'm searching for them high and low—I'm searching for them early and late. I don't mind my cottage. I don't mind my childer. I don't mind anything, but just to get hold of thim letters for the great professor."

"You're very kind," said Mrs. Beaufort. "My husband does want the letters."

"I know it, ma'am. I know, too, that when a gent wants a thing he wants it so bad that he must 'ave it. Poor folks like us we 'as to do without, but gents—they gets what they wants. That's mortal true."

"You're a very kind woman," said Mrs. Beaufort.

"I don't think, ma'am, ef I was you," suddenly interrupted Hephzibah, "I'd talk no more to Mrs. Heavyfoot—her settin' in your presence and you standin'. Ef you'll go back to the drawing-room, I'll bring you your cup of arrowroot. Do, please, ma'am."

But Mrs. Beaufort looked annoyed. "I shall do as I wish," she said, haughtily.

"A nice way for a gel to talk to you, ma'am," said Mrs. Heavyfoot, who saw a possible opening for pushing her daughter into Hephzibah's place and turning Hephzibah out. "Now, ef I was a lady, which I ain't, I'd no more put up with that kind of talk than I'd fly. Ain't you the mother of the most beautiful young gent in the world, and that brat of a girl she talks as she do and you puts up with it. Ma'am, its you that 'as the beautiful spirit. Now, ef my daughter was here——"

"Which she won't be," said Hephzibah. "So, now, ma'am, will you kindly go back to the drawing-room."

If Mrs. Beaufort had been a stronger-minded woman, she would have left the kitchen, but as it was, she sank into a chair and began to talk to Mrs. Heavyfoot again.

"Your life must be a very interesting one," she said.

"It be that, ma'am. It 'aves it ups and it's downs—it 'aves its luck, bad and good. It twists everyway, so to speak, but I'm all for you and Mr. Patrick and when they say things agen him in Hartley, its myself that's up in arms."

"They say things against my son," cried Mrs. Beaufort. "How dare you allude to such things to me. They say things against Captain Beaufort?"

"Oh, ma'am, I'm sure I beg your pardon, I don't mean nothing, I don't really. Nobody could speak against such a beautiful young gent as that."

"Well, then, my good woman, don't talk to me any longer. I ought not to have spoken to a woman like you. Hephzibah knew better. I lost my dignity when I spoke to you."

Then she turned very slowly, her sweet little figure looking as it had never looked before, almost like the Madonna in its beauty, in its simple grandeur. She quietly opened the kitchen door and went out.

"I 'a done for myself," said Mrs. Heavyfoot. "You must get me out o' this, Hephzie."

"I'm not goin' to trouble to get ye out of it," said Hephzie. "I knowed well ye'd do it. Go arter them Simpsons—and do your evil best with them. Clear away from here—that's all I got to say."

CHAPTER XIV

Patrick Beaufort was once more back in London. He had secured sufficient money, notwithstanding his remarks to the contrary, to clear himself from any chance of being cashiered; he had paid his debts of honour, he had meant to pay some more debts which were not debts of honour, debts to struggling tradespeople who badly needed the money which the ambitious, foolish, vain young man owed them, debts for dress suits here and dress suits there, for the best style of trousers, of coats, of waistcoats, of hats; debts, in fact, of the sort which young men of his calibre would contract, debts also for dinners, gay dinners, sparkling dinners, which he gave to the ladies whom he admired. He was a great admirer of the female sex was Patrick Beaufort, he always had one girl or one lady in tow, so to speak. He saw her, he fell in love with her for the time being, he loaded her with presents—those sort of people expect, well—jewellery, dinners, boxes at the theatre, boxes at the opera, all kinds of amusements. They require, in short, all those things which run up bills, but Patrick did not mind; those bills at least, could wait. If Elizabeth had been anything like what she ought to be, he would not have been like this. He could have paid his account at the Savoy, he could have paid his account at the Carlton, he could have paid a good deal, at least, of his jeweller's bill. That was rather heavy; jewels were so confoundedly dear. How he wished that he might give his mother's jewels to the lady of his love! She was so beautiful, and she would look so nice in them, and she admired old-fashioned things.

Her name was Alice Stanhope. She was a person without much character, she was a married woman, who cared little or nothing for her husband, was highly pleased to go about in the world and to be seen there with the handsome, dashing young officer, Patrick Beaufort. She liked nothing better and, truth to tell, her husband was the sort of man who did not mind. He went his way, she went hers, she belonged alas! to a very numerous class in London in these days. She did not mind the fact that she belonged to this class, she did not consider it in the leas.. She liked to dress showily, she liked to point to the lovely bracelet which Patrick had given her, she liked him to whisper in her ear, to say soft nothings, pretty, feathery kind of things, that went in at one ear and out at the other. She was married, she had no intention of giving Patrick the most remote handle to disgrace her name or position, but a flirtation with him was all very well; it was, in short, delightful. And he—he did his best, he enjoyed himself, he was quite happy—but if only Elizabeth had been different! Elizabeth, however, was herself and nothing would change her.

One day he had taken Mrs. Stanhope to the Carlton for supper. The Savoy was beginning to press him for *something* on account, he had presented a five pound note, which was scornfully returned.

" We must have,' 'said the manager to the young man, " at least fifty pounds by this day fortnight, or we cannot accommodate you any further, Captain Beaufort."

Beaufort said, with an angry flush and a flash in his dark eyes:

" So much the worse for yourselves."

" I could not run the Savoy on your terms, Captain Beaufort," replied the manager, " whatever you may say to the contrary."

So Captain Beaufort was again being pressed for money and on this special occasion he took the lady of his choice to the Carlton; the Carlton had not begun to press yet, it would very soon, he owed quite three hundred pounds there, but, of course, Elizabeth would help him. He would write to her and ask her for the Lord's sake to send him some of the money she had got for Swift-as-the-wind. He thought as he was driving with his fair companion to the Carlton, after they had enjoyed a delightful theatre together, he thought of Elizabeth and wondered and wondered *why* she had sold her beautiful horse. " There's a mystery about Elizabeth, he said to himself, " there's no doubt whatsoever on that point. There's a mystery— I must get a handle to it, and then I can manage her."

" What are you thinking of, Captain Beaufort ? " said Mrs. Stanhope, when they found themselves tête-à-tête at a small table. It was fancifully decorated with a little electric lamp and some flowers by the lady's plate and some more by the gentleman's. " You are not a bit interesting," she continued, " you are dull and stupid. I shall ask Mr. Anstruther to take me out to dinner next time, he is always begging and imploring of me to do so, and so I will—I shall just avail myself of his attentions. You are handsome—I admit that—but you are nothing else—you have no money, you know— why haven't you any money ? "

" My dear lady, my sweet lady, do you think I like being without money ? "

"Well, well, it's all the same to me. Anstruther has half-a-million at least and he can positively cover me with jewels. But, Patrick, I like you best, and why don't you give me a diamond ring? I saw one at Storr and Mortimer's the other day, it's only five hundred pounds—a mere trifle—you might buy it for me. My husband is having a fine time with—oh, I won't mention any names!— but it is rather dull for me to go out with a man who is absorbed in melancholy thoughts."

"I am sorry," said Beaufort, "I have a good deal to worry me just at present. The fact is, I am afflicted with a sister."

"Afflicted with a sister? What a very, *very* strange thing to say!"

"It is true, all the same, Alicia," said Patrick, bending towards her, "my sister is very rich."

"Your sister rich, and you are poor? how do you make that out?"

"Well, just as a matter of pounds, shillings and pence; she's not rich, according to our favourite Anstruther, but she's rich in one way. She has at least several hundred pounds, which she will not even let me see the colour of. I went down to the miserable place where my father, the professor, lives, and I did what I could with Elizabeth."

"Elizabeth," said Mrs. Stanhope, "what a pretty, uncommon name. I used to hate it when I was a child, but I admire it now. Is your sister handsome?"

"Oh, very."

"Then why don't you bring her up to town and do a brother's part for her? Why, if she's handsome and rich she might make no end of a fine match. I tell you what it is. For your sake, Patrick, I'd place her under my wing, and take her about with me. She'd have, of course, to provide herself with suitable clothes, but I'd soon marry her off. There are heaps of men looking for wives in the present day; there are men who want rich wives, there are men who don't care anything at all about riches, provided they get handsome wives, and you say your sister is handsome."

"You can judge for yourself," said Patrick. He slipped his hand into his waistcoat pocket and took out a little photograph of Elizabeth. It was in a case and lying beside it was his mother's most valuable diamond ring. It was her engagement ring, the one which her husband had given her on that happy day when they had plighted their troth and vowed each to be faithful to the other, and each had been truly faithful to the other through the long years. No thought of disloyalty had come into their hearts and their child Elizabeth took after them.

"But do let me look at that ring—what a beauty! what a love! what a darling!" said Mrs. Stanhope.

"I am glad you admire it, it belongs to my mother."

"Oh, oh, Patrick!—and you said, you swore that you hadn't a penny in the world! and you have got this! Why, I don't know what it would fetch! Give it to me, Patrick, give it to me, and I won't go with Mr. Anstruther: I will stay with you, Patrick, I will, I will!"

CHAPTER XV

AFTER a certain exceedingly worldly fashion Mrs. Stanhope looked very beautiful as she spoke. Her eyes were bright blue—like china—her hair was a very rich shade of gold. Those who knew her best, knew also that her hair was apt to assume many tinges according to the prevailing mode. At present it was golden, with a touch—only a touch—of red, which gave it a very brilliant appearance. Her cheeks were powered as a matter of course, and were also faintly, very faintly, rouged.

Mrs. Stanhope looked exactly like the woman she really was—one without morals—one without any idea of behaving correctly; she cared little or nothing of what the world thought of her, always provided she could keep that little measure of self-respect, which would enable her to enjoy a certain class—by no means a high class—of London society.

She fiddled now with the lovely ring—the little ring which was surely the symbol of all love and purity. She slipped it on her finger and watched the diamonds shine and glitter.

"No, I cannot part with that ring," said Patrick—who never admired her more, or, at the same time, hated her more profoundly.

She looked up—startled by his tone and by the down-right anger in his great black eyes. A natural colour now mounted to her cheeks, an expression of fury trembled round her full, red lips.

"Take it," she said, flinging it back to him. He caught it and slipped it with a sense of relief into his breast pocket.

"Yes—take it," she continued with a taunting laugh, "and I will tell that fat millionare, Archibald Anstruther that I will dine with him to-morrow night at the Ritz—It is twice the fun at the Ritz and we can go to the Empire— or some such place afterwards. Of course I know that poor old Archie is ugly—but they say—those in the *know*, that in a week's time you do not know an ugly man from a handsome one—as handsome as you are Pat, when you do not wear that detestible sneer. Of course I know you are splendidly handsome generally. At times your face is like a dream—but I have a strong suspicion that your pockets are *not* lined with gold, poor old dear—and I want gold more than any thing else in the world. Now let me have a squint at that young girl's photograph."

Patrick, against his will, handed the wicked woman the little case—She gazed for half-a-minute at the tranquil, serene, noble face. She felt at that moment that she was darkness looking at light. She closed the little case with a sharp snap and gave it back to Patrick.

"I don't think," she said, "that that girl would suit me. She—I know her sort."

"You'd better not speak against her, she's my sister," replied Patrick. He then sat perfectly quiet without speaking at all. Mrs. Stanhope looked at him; there was a change in this young man which she could not account for. Was it possible that her fascinations were failing in their effects? Was it possible that he no longer cared for her, as he used to do? She suddenly bent towards him.

"Show me that photograph again," she said.

He hesitated for a moment. His first feeling was to refuse. To show light to darkness was even against *his* inclination. But after a moment's hesitation, impelled by her undoubted charm, he took the photograph out again and put it into her hand.

"She is good, you can see that," he said.

"Yes, I can see it very well. If—if I take your sister about in London, if I ask her to visit me at my house in Audley Place, if I do all that one woman can do for another, will you give me that diamond ring ? There! that's a fair bargain, is it not ?"

"It is a bargain that cannot be contemplated," replied Beaufort. He was not impressed in any way by Mrs. Stanhope's remarks. He liked her, nay more, he had a certain craving for her society, which he could not resist, but— his mother's engagement ring, his mother! If there was anyone in all the world who truly loved him it was that little, frail, delicate, sweet woman who lived far away in the wilds of Craig Moor. No, no, he could not part with the ring. He could give it to a good girl, to a girl whom he loved and whom he would not be ashamed to bring some day to his mother and say—" she is my wife "—but this woman! He rose abruptly.

"There's one thing and only one thing to be said," he remarked, "and it is this—that if you were to ask Elizabeth fifty times over to visit you, she would refuse. She is in her own way a person of importance. She gets her pictures of the moors, the moor ponies, the moor men and women, into the academy year after year, and year after year they are sold without the slightest difficulty. What she gets for them I don't know, but I should fancy a large sum. In addition she is a marvellous musician. She plays the organ so magnificently that she is employed by some of our greatest organists to write fresh music for them; they pay her for her music—in short, she is far too busy to come to you. Your life would not suit her, your ways would not suit her, in fact, nothing about you would suit her. You do suit *me* uncommonly well; but my sister, she is quite different."

"As you please," said Mrs. Stanhope, turning purple with rage, "I don't want to have anything to do with this model young lady, and a professional—a professional is not in the least in my line, so no more about her. I am tired, I want to go home." And Patrick took her home.

While these things were happening in London Patrick was once again terribly short of money. There was the diamond ring, he had sold all the rest of the jewels, but he had kept the ring. Whenever he felt tempted to go into a jeweller's shop and see what he could get for the ring, something or someone seemed to pull him back, a voice seemed to sound in his ears. "Your mother's, your loving mother's engagement ring—*will* you, *can* you part with it?" He felt somehow that he could not, hitherto he had felt this. The people at the Savoy must wait, they must press a little harder. Oh, they could do him no harm, and he had been truly careful with regard to debts of honour ever since his last visit to Craig Moor.

But at Hartley, at Hartleypool, in the home of professor and Mrs. Beaufort, matters were moving in a direction which would have much astounded that astute young officer had he known enough about them, for Mrs. Heavyfoot was not, to use an old adage, allowing the grass to grow under her feet. She was working day and night to find the Simpsons; she could not, try as she would, discover their abode, therefore she was more or less in a state of despair. The two pounds a month was regularly paid by Elizabeth, but that seemed so little and twenty-five pounds was scarcely worth taking, and the glow of pleasure at the thought of having "Miss" locked up did not appear so joyous when it came to the point. But on a certain evening towards the end of April, when Adrian Trent must be quite safe—Elizabeth always had that feeling in her heart now—when he must be quite safe, having left Hartleypool at least a couple of months ago—the man Heavyfoot came into his cottage with a frown between his brows. It was a very ominous frown, it was a frown so ominous, so portentous, that his children, instead of running to him as they generally did, crept away from him and, on the whole, preferred their mother to their father on this occasion. He hardly touched his supper, he let it go—in fact, as soon as ever it was over, he turned to his wife.

"Send the brats to bed," he said.

"What's the matter with ye, Jim? Whyever are ye so—so spiteful—like? Not even that bit of a Lizzie can please ye to-night," remarked Mrs. Heavyfoot.

"Send the brats to bed," said the man again. "If ye don't I'll go to the "Green Dragon," and ye know what that means."

"Ye'd best go to bed, childer," said their mother. She was a little awed by her husband's manner, she was, if the truth must be told, also a trifle frightened. The children went upstairs one by one, they crept into their beds, Lizzie cried a little, daddy was never like that as a rule, daddy always kissed his little Lizzie, whoever else he didn't kiss. What was the matter with daddy? Juliana, another girl, told her to "shut up." But this did not prevent Lizzie from crying very quietly, very softly, under the sheets. Meanwhile husband and wife were closeted together downstairs.

"What?" said the woman—"what? ye don't want me to wash the bits of plates afore ye begin to talk? Whatever has come to ye, Jim?"

ELIZABETH'S PRISONER

"I'll tell you—you must get me out of it."

"Well, my man, I was always a good wife to ye."

"That you were, Maria," was his response. Then he said, after a pause—"I've done a fearful thing, and if it's known I'm a ruined man. *The children 'll have nothing to eat ; the children 'll have nothing to eat.*"

"God in heaven, stop making that awful remark!" cried Mrs. Heavyfoot. "Haven't I been tramping and tramping, and doing my level best for the children? Whatever have ye gone and done, Jim?"

"I'll tell you, my woman, what I've gone and done. I was desperate—I—I couldn't help myself—it come on me like a lightning flash! I saw a bit o' money in the governor's room—he sent me to his private room to fetch some things he wanted, some books, if ye must know, and there was, lying on his table, ten golden sovereigns, and I wanted the money that bad, that bad, Maria, that I took it, I took it and I paid off a man who's been plaguing me for months and months. He may never think it was me, for I left the matter so that most likely the blame might fall on Joe—the new hand they have in the prison. No one likes Joe and that's the truth, and my hope is that it'll fall on him. He was sent into the governor's study after me, Maria, and if it falls on him, well and good, but there's great, great danger. Can ye raise ten pounds, so that I may pay it back, Maria, my woman?"

"And what if I don't?" asked Mrs. Heavyfoot.

"Then the children 'll have no bread to eat. That was why I couldn't kiss Lizzie to-night; I couldn't look at 'em, I couldn't look at any of 'em, I seemed to see 'em getting thinner and thinner and more and more peaky, and I couldn't bear it!—and here I am, here I am! I've stolen money; and I'll be disgraced and put into prison. Can ye help me, Maria, my woman?"

"It'll all depend on whether the blame is laid on Joe or not."

"But if it's not laid on Joe it'll be put on me, and I can't stand it! I'll run away this blessed night."

"And fasten it on yourself," said Mrs. Heavyfoot, "a nice sort of man you be, Jim, I must say I admire your character."

"Well, woman, can ye help me?"

"I dunno, I dunno—oh, God, help us, we're in a nice state! I, the wife of a common thief! God help us, we're in a nice state!"

CHAPTER XVI

LIZZIE could not sleep; she dropped asleep, it is true, but she woke again immediately. When she woke, she cried: "Daddy, daddy, daddy, one kiss, one kiss!"—and then she began to sob, and then she dropped into an uneasy, night-marey sort of sleep again, but it wasn't a real sleep, it was the sort that meant shadows under the eyes in the morning, it was the sort that would wear the small child into a shadow, the shadow that her father contemplated when he could not kiss her.

Mrs. Heavyfoot came upstairs very late to bed, she had been talking to her husband, nobody knew what they said to each other. But as she passed the door where the children slept, she heard a quick little suppressed sob. As a rule she never dreamt of noticing when the children cried, she said it was very bad to notice them, it would be a hardening process to let them fight through their childish troubles. She was not the sort of woman to pamper and pet, she was the last to do that. Heavyfoot was silly about the little girl, even Juliana, big girl that she was, fit to be in a place now, fit to be with " miss," and her father and mother, even Juliana he took notice of, but if Mrs. Heavyfoot cared for any of her children, it was the boys. But this sob came from the tiny room where the girls slept together. She stood still on the landing; she felt bewildered enough, poor woman, and that sob went to her heart. She did not know she had a heart, but it was touched by that sob. She opened the door very softly, an eager little voice said:

" Is that you, daddy ? "

" No, t'ain't, t'ain't ; you go to sleep, Lizzie."

" I want daddy to kiss me, I want daddy to kiss me, I want, I want—— " a great flood of tears fell from the child's eyes. For a wonder the woman was softened; she took the little creature in her arms; she was her youngest, she wrapped a large grey shawl round her and carried her straight downstairs.

" Here," she said, " here—she won't sleep all night ef you don't kiss her. Kiss her and let her go to sleep."

The man, left alone for the first time, was going to the cupboard where the whiskey bottle was hidden. He scowled, but one look at Lizzie softened him.

" Oh, ye poor little thing," he said, " ye poor little thing ! "—and he took her in his arms and kissed her with passion, almost with ferocity ;

he kissed her over and over. " My poor Lizzie, my poor Lizzie, ye'll never think bad of your daddy, will ye, Lizzie mine ? "

" Never, never, *never*, daddy. Oh, daddy, you does love your little Lizzie ? "

" I does, my child, I does."

" There now, kiss her again, and I'll take her up to bed," said the mother, " and you come to bed, for the Lord's sake, Jim, or the morning will be on us before you've got into bed."

Lizzie, quite satisfied now by her father's kisses, by her restoration to favour, kissed her mother too, cuddled in a comfortable way into the bed which she shared with Juliana, and went off into profound slumber. Nothing mattered, after all, it was only that daddy was cross at supper, but he loved his little Lizzie, he would always love her, there was no doubt of that. She fell into the happy, dreamless sleep of an innocent child.

Meanwhile Jim Heavyfoot took two glasses of whiskey. He did not trouble to water them. He was in a state of despair. Afterwards he took a certain condiment which removed the smell of whiskey from his breath, and then, soothed by the spirit, he went upstairs and lay down beside his wife. Notwithstanding his trouble, his danger, he was soon sleeping the sleep of the just. Mrs. Heavyfoot was the one, after all, who remained awake. She was thinking. In spite of his many faults, in spite of the fact that she was not a woman of much affection, she cared for Jim, she cared for him in her rough, uncouth way; she did not want him to be put in prison. A fine crow the Jennifers and the Prices would have if her husband, her husband, Jim Heavyfoot, was arrested on the crime of theft, if he was put into prison. Oh, she could not stand it! and she could so easily get twenty-five pounds; after all, what was Miss Elizabeth Beaufort to her, compared to Jim and the children? She could get the money, she could get it to-morrow. She dared not hesitate any longer. She had just been paid her usual two pounds for her silence, that two pounds would prove Elizabeth's guilt. She always took care to mark in a little book: " Received from Miss Elizabeth Beaufort the sum of two pounds to keep silence on a certain matter connected with a felon." This book was kept carefully locked up in a small drawer upstairs. She used the two pounds to buy clothes for the children. In her way she was a good mother, at least, in her way, she was not altogether bad. She could not get another penny from Miss Beaufort for another month at least—stay—should she go to Miss Beaufort and tell her the story and ask her to give her ten pounds? That might be best, that would give her a chance. After thinking this matter over several times she decided to adopt this plan, at least first. If Miss Beaufort refused—and she was such a queer young miss— she never called her anything but "miss" now—if she refused, then she, Mrs. Heavyfoot, would feel no compunction, she would get her twenty-five pounds, she would give her husband ten pounds to put back on the governor's table, and all would be well.

Accordingly at breakfast next morning Mrs. Heavyfoot was quite cheerful. The children, even little Lizzie, went off to school, looking and feeling much as usual.

"Juliana is getting a big gell, ain't she, wife?" said the husband. "She ought to be getting a small place, a big gell ought to be getting a small place—ha! ha!—he! he!— that's a joke, ain't it, wife?"

"I don't want a small place," said Juliana "I want my father to support me."

"Ha! ha!—he! he! You'd best be looking out for a place, Juliana."

"What I was thinking was this," said Mrs. Heavyfoot, "that she ought to go to them Beauforts."

"And why? The Beauforts, they've got a very

respectable gell, Hephzibah, one of the moor gells."

" Who'd compare a moor gell—you tell me—to a gell belonging to a man employed in honourable work ?" said his wife, with a toss of her head. " I know what I know—and now, off with ye to school ! Here's yer dinner made up in this basket, eat it careful and eat it fair ; there's a lump of cheese for each of the boys and there's jam and bread for the gells. Now, off with ye, off with ye ! "

" Why are ye in such a hurry to send them off ? " asked the husband.

" Because, Jim, I want to ask ye a question."

" Well, and whatever may that be ? "

" It's this, my man. When ye took the money, might it be possible for it not to be missed for a day or so ? "

" Very possible," said the man. " I took it from under a pile of papers, and the governor, for all he's so particular about our work, he's not to say a tidy man himself. He keeps his desk shocking—that's the only word for it. How a man in his position could leave ten sovereigns under a pile of papers !—why, it mayn't be missed for three or four days."

" Then that's your hope, ain't it, Jim ? "

" It is, my woman, it is, but oh ! my best hope is that Joe will have it landed on him.

Nobody likes him, he's a sly-looking chap with a squint in one eye and red hair ; nobody likes Joe."

" Well, well, you get to your work, don't be late, for heaven's sake ! Trust to Providence and all may be well."

" Ye have a scheme in your head, old woman."

" I'm not denyin' that I have, and I'm not sayin' that I haven't."

" Well, well, give us a kiss, old woman."

She allowed him to kiss her, wiping her mouth afterwards.

" I tell you what it is, Jim, you smell of the whiskey bottle."

" No, I don't, and it's real mean of ye to say such a thing of me."

" Well, I has me doubts, and ef ye take to drink, the prison 'll reform ye fast enough, old man."

The " old man," as she called him, went out with a sulky movement. She watched him as he went down the street, soon he turned the corner and Jennifer and Price joined him ; it was full time for these three men to get to their work in the prison. There were hard times enough at Hartleypool Prison. The new men who had arrived were very hard to break in, they seemed to be without fear and without any sort of self-respect. The fact was that the escape of Adrian Trent had reached their ears, and they talked of it in low whispers when they were alone together, and Heavyfoot felt almost certain that there would be another try for an escape in a short time, and if only he could win his innings then, how fine it would be for him. He could leave the low class in which he was placed, and get into class number two, and from class number two to class number one was so easy a step; he felt sure enough that would be his reward. That would mean higher wages, a better house, a little room for Lizzie all to herself, and Jennifer and Price under him, not over him. He'd watch, he'd look out, the day was coming when his turn would arrive, when he would be the man pointed out as "that good fellow, Heavyfoot, who'd saved the prison from another disgrace."

Meanwhile Mrs. Heavyfoot put on what she called her "best dress." Her best dress was black, over it she wore a mantle trimmed with heavy bugles. These were long beads, which hung in a fringe all round the edge of the mantle; the mantle was fastened tight and secured round her neck, it had little slits at each side through which she could put her hands; she could keep them cosy and warm in that fashion. On her head she wore a bonnet which "miss" had given her some time ago; it had belonged to Mrs. Beaufort's mother, who was still alive and lived in London. It was a very neat, nice-looking bonnet, it was made of black velvet, and had wide strings which she tied under her chin in a big bow that she considered most stylish. Thus attired, she went as quickly as she could in the direction of Craig Moor. Elizabeth was certainly not expecting her that day. Mrs. Heavyfoot was about half-way to Craig Moor when it suddenly occurred to her that she would do far better for herself and her husband if she went straight to the studio; there Hephzibah would not be about, Hephzibah, whom she hated. Accordingly she turned off in that direction. She smiled to herself when she looked at the blackberry briar and thought of her own acuteness in putting the darned sock of the convict on the briar. How little Miss Elizabeth Beaufort knew how that small trick was carried out! But there was more to follow. Had she not seen the burying of the boots? Had she not followed Miss Beaufort step by step into the forest late at night? Oh yes, Miss Beaufort was altogether in her power.

By and bye she reached the studio. She was rejoiced to hear the sound of the organ. She stood for a minute and peered into the room

(ANSI and ISO TEST CHART No 2)

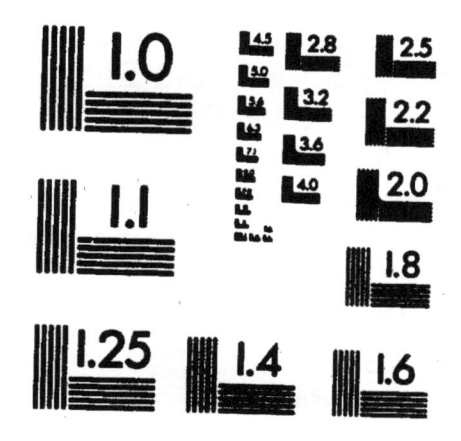

APPLIED IMAGE Inc
1653 East Main Street
Rochester, New York 14609 USA
(716) 482 - 0300 - Phone
(716) 288 - 5989 - Fax

where the girl was sitting, writing occasionally, and occasionally bringing forth from the splendid little instrument, noble notes, of noble sound. Elizabeth had no fear now, all fear was at an end. There was that dreadful woman, of course, but she could be bribed, and Elizabeth felt that she could not do better than bribe her. After a short pause, Mrs. Heavyfoot knocked sharply on the window-pane. Elizabeth started, she recognised her face; she went to the door and opened it.

"Do you want anything?" she said.

"Yes, Miss, I want ye."

"But I paid you yesterday."

"T'ain't about that, Miss, it's on another matter altogether; it's on a werry serious matter, Miss: it means for ye, and for me, and for my man Jim; it means—there, Miss, I can't speak with the wind blowing like a knife through me. May I come in, Miss? Ye've harboured worse than me in this here stoodio."

"Come in," said Elizabeth. She opened the door a little wider and the woman entered. "Take a chair," continued Elizabeth; as she spoke she pulled down the blind near the organ, she did not want anyone to see her conversing with Mrs. Heavyfoot. "Now, if you will tell me at once exactly what you want," she said, "I shall know what to do. I am in a very great hurry; I have had a letter from town requiring some music immediately, I must get it done somehow, in some fashion, to-day, and you waste my precious moments with talk. What is it you want, Mrs. Heavyfoot?"

"I want ten punds."

"Nonsense," said Elizabeth. "I am not going to be blackmailed to the extent of ten pounds; of course I won't give it."

"Werry well, Miss, I only thought I'd ask ye. It's werry important for *you*, Miss, that ye should give it, it's werry, *werry* important."

"I don't believe it," replied Elizabeth. "I gave you two pounds yesterday; I feel more and more that I did wrong ever to listen to your stories, ever to get myself into your power."

"Ay, but ye *be* in my power, Miss, ye *be* in my power," said the angry woman. "Well, well, is it ten punds, or is it nothing at all?"

"It is nothing at all," said Elizabeth.

"Ye're sartain sure on that point, Miss?"

"Yes, I am certain. I will pay you when the time comes round another two pounds; I will keep my word to the letter, but beyond that sum I will not go. That means twenty-four pounds a year, and, remember, I gave you ten pounds to start with. You will get nothing more from me, Mrs. Heavyfoot."

"Ye're sure?"

"I am certain."

"Then ye'll take the consequences."

"What do you mean?"

"Eh, eh l ye'll soon know. I won't keep ye from your work; if I was ye I'd work precious hard to-day, I'd get that thing done and send it to Lunnon town, that I would, because, because—oh, I *has me reasons!* Ye *could* have saved yourself, if ye had given me ten punds, but ye're sartain----"

CHAPTER XVII

"YES," said Elizabeth, " I am absolutely sure —I did wrong ever to listen to you and to give you any money—I blame myself exceedingly for doing so—but I certainly will not help you by so much as another penny—Now go at once please for I am exceedingly busy."

A wild uncontrollable anger filled the girl's breast.

This awful woman meant to black mail her—to make her young life not worth living. She would go home that very day and implore her father to leave " Craig Moor " ; she would even let her precious studio go—her organ could, of course, be set up for her elsewhere. She could afford the expense—for that very morning she had received orders for pictures and music which would put her in funds to the amount of a couple of thousand pounds. She had felt so light-hearted when she started for her day's work that morning—but the woman's visit was unbearable.

She went to the window to draw up the blind. Mrs. Heavyfoot was standing facing the studio; she had one great brawny hand clenched tightly

—and this hand she was shaking at Elizabeth. The look on the woman's face was perfectly awful.

"What does she mean? what does she mean? Is there danger? There can't be, she can't know anything; I have been, oh, so careful!" thought the girl. "She only wants to blackmail and I won't be blackmailed beyond the extent I spoke of."

Meanwhile Mrs. Heavyfoot, having vented her wrath on Elizabeth, turned quickly in the direction of Hartleypool prison. She was going again to the governor and she was going this time with news, yes, news which would astonish him, yes, news which would land that pretty young lady in jail. She would soon be at Holloway, from Holloway she would go to the women's prison at Chard—she would serve her time. Her conduct had been so altogether base that she would get probably from three to four years, perhaps five years, that would be a fine come-down for the gentleman, the handsome gentleman, she was sorry for him, 'pon her word she was, but there, *her* man, Heavyfoot, must be saved at any cost.

She asked to see the governor. The governor was particularly busy; when he was told that Mrs. Heavyfoot was waiting to see him a scowl came over his face.

"That woman again," he said. "If she has nothing more to say to me than she had last time, go and tell her that I am far and away too busy to be disturbed this morning."

The warder went off with the message, Mrs. Heavyfoot's reply was:

"Tell himself that I has got something of great import to relate to his highness."

Somewhat to the woman's surprise and undoubtedly to her pleasure, she was invited into the governor's private sitting-room, the very room where Heavyfoot, unlucky, miserable man, had stolen the ten sovereigns the day before. She looked anxiously at the table, but she had barely time to glance in that direction before Captain Marshall appeared.

"Well, Mrs. Heavyfoot," said Captain Marshall, speaking with some impatience, "I happen to be in a great hurry this morning—I can only give you a moment or two—say your say at once and then go—I am sorry to sound chuff but my business just at present is very arduous."

"And so is mine for that matter your mighteness," was Mrs. Heavyfoot's strange reply— Look ye here sir—yer mighteness— Short words and few is best—Give me ten pund—only ten pund for the present and I can put yer hand— yer naked hand upon the pussen what saved the base convict—the black murderer—'Adrian Trent."

"What utter nonsense you are talking! Ten pounds!

"And twenty by and bye but a tenner ull do the job for the time being. I can lay before ye, captain, proofs that ye cannot for a moment go agen. Is it to be yes or is it to be no? Ef, arter I ha' told my tale ye thinks it ain't so to speak worth the valley o' the money—why there I be! But I won't open these lips till I gets the money."

The woman looked so mysterious, her face was so flushed, her eyes so bright, and yet there was, withal, something about her which impressed in a curious way the governor of Hartleypool prison. It was, be it known to all readers, a standing disgrace to a governor of a great prison like Hartleypool, to allow one of the most noted prisoners under his care to escape from his clutches; he would gladly give, o of his own private funds, ten pounds, for th.. purpose of throwing any light on the matter.

"Well, I—I will trust you," he said. "Let me see—there ought to be ten pounds on this table, I remember putting them here yesterday."

He began to fidget about the papers, but nowhere could he find the money;

"You will excuse me for a minute, Mrs.

Heavyfoot," was his remark. He went out of the room; presently he returned with the ten pounds in loose gold, which he placed in the woman's hand. "And now I am ready to listen to your story," he said. But just at that moment, as good luck would have it, or rather bad luck, there came a tap at the door; a man called eagerly for the governor's presence. "I'm very sorry to leave you, Mrs. Heavyfoot," he said, "but I will be back in a moment, don't stir, I will be back directly. Yes, yes, James, what is it?"

He walked a little way down the corridor, talking to the man as he did so. Meanwhile Mrs. Heavyfoot, quick as thought, put the ten pounds under a stack of papers which the governor had not looked at this morning. When he came back she greeted him with a broad smile on her face.

"Men is men, and women is women," she said. "Ye don't half know how to find a thing. Now then, what do ye say to me? what do ye say to my powers of search? When I were left alone here, I said to myself—'The governor, his highness, is looking for ten punds, and he can't find it.' Did ye look under here, governor?"

"I did not," said the governor.

"Well, look now, for I don't want to have a hand in the matter."

The governor lifted a pile of papers, mostly letters and some manuscripts, for he was keeping careful notes of all that went on in the prison—there lay ten golden sovereigns.

"I'm sure I'm tremendously obliged to you," he said, "I'm very glad, because I should have been obliged to make a complete search and to have had all the people who entered my study yesterday and to-day called into my presence to account for the loss of my ten sovereigns. I drew it from the bank in order to pay some of my men and—in fact, I am greatly obliged to you. You see my weakness, Mrs. Heavyfoot. Although I believe I am a man with some powers of organisation, I am also not very tidy. I am greatly obliged."

"Ye'd best put it into your pocket, governor —your highness, I mean. And now for my story."

"Yes, for your story," said he governor of Hartleypool prison.

"Well now, ye look at this. Here it begins and here it ends." Whereupon Mrs. Heavyfoot took out of her pocket a little note book, which belonged, as a matter of fact, to Juliana, but which she had borrowed from her child. Juliana did not know why her mother wanted the book, but as she was not the least interested in it herself, having no turn for "learning," as she expressed it, she gave it to her willingly. In it Mrs. Heavyfoot had written the following facts.

"Ond the 4th of February, 18—, received from Miss Elizabeth Beaufort ten punds.

"You will excuse my writing, mister, but I ain't a scholar, and my spelling is poor."

"And why did you receive ten pounds from Miss Beaufort?" asked Captain Marshall, a queer sensation coming over him, and his heart beating a trifle faster than its wont, for he had a keen and very real admiration for the splendid girl.

"Ah, sir, now ye're coming to the pint. I got that ten punds from her because—because I knew summat that *she had done*, I knew it, and she guv' it to me to ensure my silence."

"And after taking it you have come to me to *break* your silence?" said the governor, his face turning a kind of chalky white.

"Be that as it may, sir, business is business, and I've been troubled in my mind, I have so. Miss Elizabeth Beaufort—I'll tell ye, sir—or ye'd best read for yerself."

The governor took the badly written book and read the following words:—

"February 4th. Found outside Miss
"Elizabeth Beaufort's stoodio a stocking
'belonging to one of the felons at the prison
"at Hartleypool, took the stocking and

"brought it to Miss Beaufort, Miss Beaufort "cried out when she saw it, but I said to "her—'no, no, none of this, I'll give it to ye "for a price,'—and she guv' me ten punds. "Then she promised me two punds a month "in addition ef I'd keep her secret."

"Yes, governor, yes, your highness, her secret—and yesterday was the last instalment, and every month, on the 4th of the month, I gets two punds from Miss Elizabeth Beaufort."

"But what for?" asked the governor.

"Ah, yes, what has the young lady to do with a felon's stocking, and what has she to do with a felon's boots, for I'd my suspects and I follied her. I follied her into the forest, that strip of land not very far from Craig Moor, and I seed her a-berryin' of one boot in one place, and a-berryin' of another boot in another place, and she put the soft fallen leaves—what was left of them—over the place that she dug up, and she patted it down with her trowel and her spade, and she come away. She never knew that she was watched, and I told her, and then she promised that ef I'd be true to her she'd—she'd keep her word to me, and I got my ten punds and I get my two punds a month. This is the last entry, your highness, here it is. This is the 5th of April and she guv' it to me yesterday. Now then, don't ye think there's a clue to the finding again of that felon, that murderer, h'Adrian Trent? And don't ye think that Mrs. Heavyfoot—for all ye don't like her—is a woman with brains in her 'ead, don't ye think so, governor?"

"I think you're a bad, wicked woman, and if it wasn't in the cause of the government master whom I serve, I would turn you out of this house. I trust you are mistaken. I will go and see—I will go and see Miss Beaufort. I respect her. I am sure, quite sure there is a mistake. Yes, keep your ten pounds if you must, but you won't get another penny until you produce the man, Adrian Trent."

"He's far enough away by now, sir, but he can be found with dertectives and others after him, and I think that ef I'm the means of getting him back again to 'his 'ere prison, my poor man ought to get a rise to second class.

"Don't talk of your man, leave me now, leave me, I can't stand any more of you. Go woman, go!"

The woman went; she had at least, attained her object, but the governor sank down in his chair and covered his face with his hands.

It could not be true, it could not be true! The girl had come to him, she had told him that she was nervous, that she could not bear to go to her studio on account of the felon who was at large. She was not deep, designing, it was not in her face, it was not in her way. He thought again of those noble eyes, he thought again of that music, but all of a sudden a memory came over him :

" Have you mice here, Miss Beaufort ? "— and her reply.

" I have not noticed any, if they come I must get a cat."

That little remark, so trivial in itself, troubled him immensely now. But he would go to her, whatever happened she would tell him the truth. Poor girl, poor girl, *noble* girl, whatever she did, she did from the best motive. He was more sorry for her than he could say—oh, if only he was not in government pay ! oh, if he was anything but what he was, he would let her go free, with a hearty clasp of the hand. Oh, how cruel was his task ! But there was no time to lose. Things were bad in the prison, the escape of Adrian Trent had caused a mutiny all round among the other prisoners—it must not go on. His duty to his king and his country demanded his taking this terrible bull by the horns. He rang the bell.

" Send the pony and trap round at once," he said, " I want to go for a drive."

CHAPTER XVIII

ELIZABETH BEAUFORT continued her work at her studio quite happily. She had forgotten Mrs. Heavyfoot, her strange behaviour, her strange speech, her strange look when she last beheld her. She was absorbed, absolutely absorbed in the work she was employed upon. That work occupied every faculty of mind and body, it seemed to take her completely out of herself. She wrote and then she played, she pulled out the stops, she let the glorious music fill the air, her young heart was full of the glory of the music. She had, indeed, no time to think of one like Mrs. Heavyfoot.

But suddenly, in the midst of her arduous work, for it was very arduous, as the professor who required the fugue made a special request that it should be posted to him that evening, there came a tap at her door, a singular sort of tap, and looking out she saw the prison pony trap and the governor of the prison. There was a man with him, who had knocked at the door. The governor sat quietly, huddled up a little bit in his seat. His work was more than repugnant to him, it was little short of agony. He wanted—he had a kind of impulse to ask the man, his servant, to wait a minute, he wanted to hear some more of that glorious music. It affected him. No girl who was not a good girl could play like that, could bring forth sounds like those sounds, to the glory of God. What a girl she was, how splendid, how magnificent, how he admired her, how he thought of her! He suddenly felt within his breast that if there was a woman on God's earth whom he could bring himself to marry, it would be Elizabeth Beaufort. Then he shook himself, he must pull himself together, the government required his services.

Elizabeth came to the door, she came out with a smiling face, although when she saw the governor that same face grew a little pale, only a trifle however. Its sweetness, its openness, its generosity, were all present.

"Is it you, Captain Marshall? I am very pleased to see you. Have you come to listen to my music, will you come in for a little while?"

"I will come in for a little, Miss Beaufort."

She opened the door wide, the governor turned to his servant.

"Walk the pony up and down," he said, "keep him from catching a chill. I may be occupied here for some little time."

Elizabeth heard the words and her face grew

a shade paler. She motioned the governor to a comfortable seat; there was a fire burning in the grate, she poked it into a generous blaze. It was the sort of time when you could not offer a man any sort of meal, either lunch or tea, it was, in short, about eleven o'clock in the morning. Elizabeth drew a chair forward for herself and, facing the light, faced also the governor, whom she had put on purpose with his back to the light.

"He has something he doesn't like to say to me," thought the girl. "and I will give him every advantage." She sat very still, there was always a wonderful calm about her. She never moved her hands, she had the faculty of keeping them absolutely quiet in her lap, they remained there now perfectly motionless, capable, strong, white hands, full of power, the hands, in short, of a good woman.

"Miss Beaufort," began the governor, "I have come here on a most—*most* painful errand."

"Have you, Captain Marshall? Has it anything to do with me?"

"It has, Miss Beaufort."

"Then I am sure," remarked Elizabeth, "that you will say what you have got to say as quickly and as kindly as you can. I am prepared to listen and I promise that I will tell you the truth."

"You are a splendid girl," said the governor; "it hurts me more than I have any words to express to have to speak to you as I am now about to speak, but duty is duty."

"It is, Captain Marshall, duty is always duty, and sometimes," continued the girl, "it is painful, intensely painful."

"I will tell you exactly why I have come," he remarked, and now he shuffled his chair a little and looked down, for he could not bear to meet the honest, clear gaze of her brown eyes, those eyes so different from Patrick's, so dark and yet so full, so very full of soul.

"Miss Beaufort, do you remember an occasion some months ago now when you called to see me?"

"I do," replied Elizabeth.

"You called because you said you were nervous. Your nervousness was caused—I quote your own words—by a fear that a convict who had escaped from Hartleypool prison was hiding in your studio. You begged of me to take a couple of my warders and to come myself—or to let a couple of my warders without myself come to your studio to examine it."

"I recall the circumstance perfectly," answered the girl.

"You do?—everything about it?"

"Yes, everything."

"Do you remember one remark I made?"

"What was that?" she asked.

"I said—' Have you mice in your studio, Miss Beaufort?'"

A swift colour came into the girl's face. "Yes," she said, ' I remember that, too, and I said, ' I have no mice in the studio, if I had I should keep a cat.'"

"You were nervous with regard to a man called Adrian Trent; we were searching the moors for him high and low. There was a very thick fog at the time and I took my blind pony, because he could go anywhere in the fog, I keep him on purpose for such occasions. Now, Miss Beaufort, a woman has called to see me to-day, she brought with her a memorandum, in which she states that you—you Miss Beaufort have paid her ten pounds on a certain date —and that you have further promised two pounds per month in order to ensure her silence with regard to an escaped felon—a man who received a life sentence for no less a sin than the brutal murder of a young girl not older—*if* so old as yourself. You promised her this allowance to be paid to her as stated in her memorandum on the fourth of each month just as long as she remained silent with regard to Adrian Trent. I cannot—no—I cannot believe in the truth of this awful story, for my respect for you, my admiration for you, are both of the highest—but I must confess the memorandum looks ugly—and I want to get the truth from you. Whatever you tell me I—yes—I will most solemnly and faithfully believe."

Tears—unwonted tears—sprang to Elizabeth's eyes.

"How good you are!" she said. "Allow me to say the words once—if never again—" then she rose slowly with a sort of quiet majesty—her face had turned from red to white—but now it looked calm and even indifferent. She walked to the little mantelpiece and leant her arm on it. At last she spoke.

"Was the woman's name Heavyfoot?"

"I have no right to tell you but on this occasion I will do so, she is a Mrs. Heavyfoot, wife of one of my warders, I honestly hate the woman and should be only too glad to prove her in the wrong. A word from you will be sufficient. Her story is that she cannot keep her secret any longer on her conscience. She further says that you have hidden Adrian Trent in this studio—this room which you and I searched together. I have come to ask you if her story is a lie?"

Elizabeth did not reply at once, then she

said very gravely, "Captain Marshall how long and how severe will my punishment be?"

"My God! you haven't done it! You didn't bring him here, you didn't make—make a fool of me, you didn't hide him in the studio!"

"I did, Captain Marshall, and he is safe now. I gave him sufficient money to send him—I don't know where—but I gave him enough money to escape. He has left the country, I don't know anything whatsoever about him. I am in your hands absolutely. I think I am more glad than sorry, yes, more glad than sorry. I . . I . . it was a burden on me, but I *had to do it.*"

"And why did you ask me to come here?"

"Because I thought it would put you off the trail, Captain Marshall, and now I will show you why."

She moved with her accustomed dignity and grace, she took the large picture from its place at the door of the cupboard. It was quite dry now, it was ready to be sent to the Academy, where, indeed, it was going on the following day.

"He is safe," she said, "and I don't mind for myself. Do you see?" She pushed back the revolving shutter, she showed the narrow space behind. "He was here," she said, "at the back of the picture. There is, as you may observe, ventilation at the top of this narrow space, he could breathe here. I put him here and I varnished the picture on purpose. You can look at it, it will probably be my last picture, and my fugue can never be finished. I ask you to deal very kindly with my father and my mother, I don't mind what happens to myself, I am only glad that I have been the means of saving an innocent man."

" Innocent ! " exclaimed the governor.

" Innocent," repeated the girl. " Yes," she added, " quite innocent. I never would let him tell me his story, I wish now I had, but I wouldn't listen—to look in his face was enough. He did what he did *for another*. I will not tell you the name of the other, for that would be betraying his life work. I am ready to go with you. *I am your prisoner*."

" Upon my word, I never was so upset in the whole course of my life ! " exclaimed Captain Marshall. " Oh ! oh ! it will go terribly against you ! "

" It will go against me," said Elizabeth, " for I shall, whenever I am called into court, confess freely that I have done it. I will confess that I saved a good man from an unjust fate. It will not kill me to go to prison for his sake. Listen to me—I shall go gladly, I shall confess all that I have done, I shall say that I took him in and kept him here when he was at the last gasp of starvation—I brought you here in order to make all things safe for him while he was obliged to remain here. Do you remember asking me about mice? I was playing for you—and my music upset him—so he moved slightly—I ought not to have played—I deceived you altho' I respect you more than all men on earth except my dear old father and my prisoner. Having provided him with an outfit I took him to London under a false name. I gave him a ticket for a foreign land also under the same false name. I am not bound to tell you the name he travelled under, nor the vessel he sailed in, nor the country he went to. These are my secrets and his and two or even three years longer under punishment will be nothing to me. I will *not* betray our mutual secret. As to the stocking—doubtless Mrs. Heavyfoot has told you about that. I am sure she put it there herself—for I perfectly remember burning two stockings. But enough of her. She is a cruel, a bad woman. I would rather be in my place than in hers. I ought never to have allowed her to blackmail me. When I had given my prisoner time sufficient to escape, I ought to have gone to you and taken my punishment. I am sorry I was so weak as almost to dread it—but believe me I do not dread it now—I take it now willingly.

I am your prisoner—take me—I am ready —only deal as kindly as you can with the dear old professor and my mother."

The governor never felt so near tears in his life. It was just at that moment that a man from the prison came and knocked at the door. Captain Marshall motioned to Elizabeth to stay in the background. He went out holding the door of the studio behind him. A smart-looking warder put a telegram into the governor's hand. All those present noticed how the governor's fingers shook as he tore it open.

The words within were few.

"*Come at once to Trent Lodge near Winchester to hear dying deposition of Valentine Trent who is real murderer of Lucy Carr, and whose brother, Adrian, took his place and confessed to the crime to save their mother who loved her younger son best.*"

CHAPTER XIX

It is necessary, for the purposes of this story, to go back a few eventful months, and thus explain the real motive of Adrian Trent. The home of the Trents at this time was a large and expensive house, not far from Winchester—that town of beauty and history. The house was built by the late Mr. Trent, a very wealthy West Indian merchant, who spent the latter years of his life in making Trent Lodge as beautiful as excellent taste and unlimited money could make it. He had married a fashionable lady of the gay world, whom at first he loved—but alas! long before his death he thoroughly hated her. He discovered her shallowness and her want of principle. She was not unfaithful to him in deed, but she undoubtedly was in thought. He himself was a singularly upright man—singularly brave and manly in the best acceptation of the word. He could not even think an untruth. Alas! Mrs. Trent could, and did, pour out lies like water.

They had two sons, with only one year between them.

Adrian, the eldest, took after his father, both in appearance and character. He had the same well-opened straight eyes, that seemed to read you through. Valentine, on the contrary, had all his mother's smallnesses. As a little child he was very delicate, and there were many fears expressed for his life. Perhaps this was one of the reasons why Mrs. Trent so much preferred him to her splendid, handsome, eldest son, Adrian. She liked to pet and shield him, while Adrian required no petting from anyone. He stood, as soon as nature permitted, on his own sturdy legs, looked at the world out of his bold fearless eyes, and adored his father. That love was abundantly returned. The child and the man were always together. Trent taught his manly little son to ride, to fish, to swim. He imparted other knowledge into the lad, who received it as an open book.

Thus while Trent the elder and young Adrian enjoyed themselves over every imaginable manly sport, and the boy grew in beauty and manhood every day, young Valentine, with his weak blue eyes and long golden curls, sat by his mother's side, arrayed in velvet and fine lace. In his mother's eyes he was a little prince, whereas Adrian was a cub, a bear. But Adrian Trent the elder read the unspoken thoughts in the breast of the woman he had married, and took steps for the protection of his beloved eldest son.

He left a will in his favour. This will gave him five hundred a year during his mother's lifetime. A similar sum was settled on Valentine, with strict injunctions that the money was to be spent on his education until the time when he left Oxford, the home of learning to which the elder Trent wished both his boys to go. Their names were put down from an early age for Winchester, but only Adrian got in; the other boy was, therefore, to be sent by his mother to Rugby or Harrow, not to Eton. When the education of both boys was finished they were to choose professions which their mother would help them to secure, and the five hundred a year was to continue to be paid to them as long as their mother lived. At her death the younger son was still to receive his five hundred a year, but all the rest of Trent's very valuable property, amounting to many thousands, and including Trent Lodge and adjoining property, was to be strictly entailed on Adrian, and thus was to pass from him with certain legacies, specially provided for, to his own eldest son, should he marry, as Trent earnestly hoped he would, at an early age.

This was the nature of the will, and Adrian Trent the elder must have had a premonition that his own death would be sudden and painless, for he was found dead in his bed one summer's morning, and the post-mortem examination pronounced his death to be caused by an affection of the heart of long standing. Mrs. Trent did not mourn for the loss of that best of men, her husband, but she did howl and declaim mightily when the highly respectable firm of solicitors in Winchester read aloud to her the contents of the will. Hitherto she had borne with Adrian, but from this moment she very honestly hated the boy.

He was at a preparatory school for Winchester at the time, and came rushing home to her, his little round boyish face bathed in profound grief. He did not know about the will and cared less. His father, his best beloved father, was dead. At sight of his mother's very manifest trouble he tried hard to comfort her. She pushed him from her, her face purple with passion.

"Do not come to me with your honeyed words, Adrian," she said. "Your father has left everything to you—every farthing—and my own precious Val is practically penniless——"

"Oh! mother, I—I do not really care for the money; Val may have it *all*, only love me, mother dear, and let me comfort you."

"*You* comfort me?" was the angry woman's reply. "I tell you that at the present moment I absolutely hate you. Oh! the cruel injustice. Oh! my little Val, my little darling Val."

"Mother! indeed he may have the money—all the money. It is about father that I cannot help crying."

"Get out of my sight, child, the will cannot be altered, and my boy is a beggar."

This was the beginning of sad days for Adrian. He was far too young to understand the value of money. He went, however, small boy that he was at the time, to ask Messrs. Dane and Fairweather to explain to him the meaning of his father's will.

"It makes poor mother *so* unhappy," said the little fellow, "that, if you please, I want it changed. I suppose I need not take the money unless I like. I want to go into a great, grand profession, or I wish to explore the world. Mother says that I shall be rolling in horrid money, and Val will just be a beggar. Please, indeed, I want Val to have the money."

"In the first place," said Mr. Dane, who took a great interest in the handsome boy, "the will of your late father cannot possibly be changed, nor will it come into effect, as far as the bulk of the property is concerned, during your mother's life-time. The interest on a large sum has been set aside for her use—although she cannot touch the capital—but she is allowed to live at Trent Lodge, and to use the furniture, and the grounds will be kept up for her during her lifetime. When she dies you get the place and grounds and property, and your father wished his great property to be strictly entailed—with the exception of ten thousand pounds—on your eldest son, and so on, he hoped, for generations. Now that is talking a long way ahead, my little man. I am glad you are returning to school to-morrow. Your brother accompanies you. As to his being a beggar, I cannot see it, for as long as your mother lives you will each have five hundred a year, which will be spent partly on your education. What is over will be put in trust for you both when you come of age. At your mother's death your younger brother will still have five hundred a year paid to him quarterly for his life. Should he die before you, that sum is to be added to your property. A similar sum will be settled on you during your mother's lifetime, *or* until you are twenty-five years of age, *or* unless your mother marries again. In either of these cases the entire vast property goes to you when you are twenty-one. It is a very large property, Adrian, but for the present you and your brother possess, under guardians, five hundred a year each. I cannot call the man or boy who possesses five hundred a year a *beggar*."

"Oh! no, of course not," answered Adrian. "It is a very large sum indeed, in fact, quite an enormous sum. At least, *I* call it so. Poor mother must have misunderstood—I *am* so pleased. I'll explain to dear mother. I suppose—I suppose——" his young voice shook a trifle "—that her great, *great* loss in father's death, dulled her brain, as most surely it has mine. Thank-you so much for explaining everything to me, and for not treating me as a child."

"Dear little chap, fine little chap," said Dane to his partner, when the boy had dashed away almost as quickly as he had rushed in.

All these things happened long years ago. Adrian got over the first frantic grief of his childhood, but in some strange way the more his mother hated him, the more did he pity and love her. His love grew into a silent sort of deep passion. He never spoke of it, but it shone out of his great dreamy eyes. His love was largely mixed with pity. He hated to be richer at any time than his brother. He almost loathed the thought of one day being a very rich man. Meanwhile he grew in all that was great and noble. He was a fine athlete, and was popular at Winchester for his cricket and football, in both of which exercises he largely excelled. The boys found in him the sort of sympathetic comrade whom schoolboys most admire. The masters adored him for his modesty, and for his fine and really remarkable powers of mind. They knew well that young Trent would add glory to the great school some day. At nineteen he had won the first Balliol Scholarship of the year, but, although his talents were so brilliant, he looked younger than his years. This effect was caused by his singular modesty. He was now a sturdy, handsome youth.

It might truly be said of him in Newbolt's celebrated lines, that through all and every condition of life he would : " *Play up ! play up ! and play the game !* "

Little did he guess, in his brilliant early manhood, *what* that game was going to be, and what lay before him. He was, at this time, a very sturdy handsome lad, with eyes that looked straight through you, and were themselves of the deepest blue-grey. His eyebrows were thick and black. He had very straight features, and a singularly firm and beautiful mouth. There was a cleft in his chin, which was slightly protruding, and he always wore his black hair very short. His forehead was broad and full. He held himself like a young soldier. His height was just above six feet—his shoulders were very square and broad. He was muscular and athletic. In short, it would be difficult to find anywhere a finer specimen of young manhood than Adrian Trent.

At Winchester he was beloved, not only because of his talents, which were abundant, but on account of his sunny smile and good nature, his want of self-consciousness, and his earnest desire to help other boys who were in distress. In consequence the boys could not be jealous of him, and the masters, one and all, adored him as the sort of young fellow who would add to the glory and honour of the great school. He won his scholarship with perfect ease, and his desire was, after he left Oxford, to try either for the Diplomatic Service, or the Indian Civil Service. But this wish on his part, Mrs. Trent, aided by Valentine, opposed with all the strength of an obstinate, weak nature. She announced that she had a perfect right to arrange for the future of her sons, and w Valentine should go into the army, Adrian would obtain, through relations of her's, a post as clerk in a flourishing city house.

But Adrian was the sort of man who hated city life, and the bare idea of the confinement of the desk was odious to him. He loved adventure, he knew well that he was really rich, and his desire at present was to join an expedition to one of the Poles, but there was one very strange thing about him, he could not account for it himself, but it was there. He had loved his father—God alone knew how much he loved that precious father—but it seemed to young Adrian that the mother, who did not take the least interest in him, had been left in his care by his father. It was his duty—his pleasure—to give her that love which she had lost when his father—that man of men—died. He felt that he stood in his father's place to his mother.

Meanwhile Mrs. Trent put up with him, although she never pretended to understand him. The only love she had ever given to anyone was bestowed upon Valentine. She loved Valentine much more passionately after the contents of the will were made known to her. Her poor Val! Her ill-treated—her cruelly-used child! Her beggar-boy, as she called him.

Valentine, as a small child, was both delicate and sly. Mrs. Trent, of course, never perceived the slyness, and she adored the little fellow all the more for his delicacy. She called Adrian coarsely strong. She spoke of this noble boy as rough and uncouth. Adrian never appeared to mind. He would have given his brave young heart away to please his mother.

He and Val were not in the same school, but they both went up to Oxford at the same time, Val being a year the younger. Val had obtained no scholarship, but he was admitted after some scruples, to Exeter College. It was then that the brothers first saw much of each other, and Adrian did all that man could to shield Val from temptation.

As the years flew on, Valentine grew slyer and less handsome. He developed immoral tastes and ran up debts to an unlimited extent. It is an old saying that love is blind, and Mrs. Trent never noticed the weak mouth and the receding chin. She managed to pay all Valentine's debts, and when he told her that he wished to enter the army, she wept with joy at the thought of his uniform.

By this time Adrian had run his brilliant course. In his finals he obtained a double first. The Master of Balliol looked on him with deep affection, the dons, one and all, adored him, the men of his year could not do enough for him. But no one looked with admiration at poor Valentine, who, owing to his lack of talent, and his idle ways, barely scraped through his examinations.

When Adrian finished his course with glory

at the Sheldonian, the master sent for him and asked him what he intended to do in the future.

Adrian's dark face coloured very slightly, then he gave the man whom he loved one of his wonderful straight glances, and remarked simply:

"I am to work my way up as a clerk in the city of London."

"You in the city!" cried the master in horror.

"Yes, sir."

"Trent, tell me, is this your own wish?"

Trent remained silent for a moment, then, being unable to tell a lie, he spoke the truth.

"No, master, I do not wish it."

"Then, why, in the name of heaven, do you throw yourself away?"

"My mother desires it."

"Your mother desires *such* a career for *such* a brain—for *such* a man. Forgive my asking a plain question. I understand that your father is dead. Is your mother poor?"

"By no means," said Trent, then he added, speaking simply, "I shall be rich—very rich myself when I am five-and-twenty. I have had the great misfortune, master, of losing my father, and my desire now is to please my mother. She wants my brother Valentine to enter the army."

"Your brother? Is Trent, of Exeter, your brother?"

"Yes, master."

"Well said the master. "Valentine Trent is to be put over your head. I should advise, *you*, Trent, to give him a pretty sound hint. I have no right to speak, for he does not belong to this college, but unless he is exceedingly careful I have good reasons for knowing that he has little or no chance of finishing his career at Oxford. The fact is this. Oxford does not want men of his sort. Trent, my dear lad, I take a deep interest in you—we all do at Balliol —now oblige me with your mother's address."

Trent gave it, but unwillingly.

On the following day, Mrs. Trent, who was expecting both her sons home, Adrian for a brief holiday before he took up his abode in the city, Valentine for the whole of the vac, received a letter from the master of Balliol.

Its contents were as follows:—

"Dear Madam,

"I trust you will forgive a stranger addressing you; and yet I do not consider myself quite a stranger, for I know you of course through your admirable and most brilliant son."

Mrs. Trent paused for a moment to draw in these delightful words. Could the Rector of

Exeter be alluding to her Valentine—the pride of her heart? But glancing at the printed address on the top of the notepaper, her momentary delight vanished. She continued, however to read, stirring her coffee and sipping it as she did so.

"most brilliant son," she resumed. "Your mother's heart must indeed have filled with pride when you saw that Adrain Trent has been awarded the highest honour possible by his Alma Mater. He is a double Honours man and stands first in the list. All his friends and all my friends take the deepest interest in this gifted youth's future. His talents are so great and his motives so noble that there is no high post to which he need not eventually aspire; but, madam, I questioned him yesterday, and, to my unbounded astonishment, he informed me that although he would be a rich man by and bye, he was going by your desire into the city.

"I have nothing whatever to say against the city, nor against the honest and brave men who earn their bread there, but believe me, it is not the place for Adrian Trent. He could, with the utmost ease, get a post in the Diplomatic Service or the Indian Civil. These would be wider and greater courses for him, far better than the city. I understand from his own lips that gold he does not need. We love him in old Balliol, not only for his mental gifts, but for his clean, good life, for his straight conduct, for his noble character. Do not deliberately spoil the prospects of such a man. In the name of Balliol I beg you carefully to consider my letter. Pending your reply I have invited Trent to spend the next few days with me.

"Yours, dear madam, with all congratulations,
" JOHN SHEEN,
" Master of Balliol."

What effect this letter might have had on Mrs. Trent it is difficult to say. She loved Valentine—she did not love Adrian. There was something about him too straight for her crooked nature. It is true she would like to be proud of him, but she only managed to be jealous. Still the words of the Master of Balliol impressed her and perhaps, if she listened to his words, Adrian might be able to help her precious Val by and bye.

She did not quite know how to reply to the master's letter and matters might have arranged themselves very differently if she had not just at that very moment perceived another letter lying under a pile of bills close to her plate. This letter was also dated from Oxford—she knew the writing. She had seen it several times before. Her heart beat a little faster than usual and she hoped that here at last might be good news of her darling, her Val. She opened the letter of the Rector of Exeter College eagerly. She arranged herself with a happy sense of content to read it. The words were firm and very much to the point.

"Exeter College,
"Oxford.

"Madam,

"It is my painful duty to have to inform you that your son, Valentine Trent, has been sent down—in other words *expelled*. Madam, we cannot do with this young gentleman here any longer. His hopeless debts with the tradespeople, his equally hopeless debts of so-called honour—by this I mean debts incurred by horse-racing and cards, his incorrigible idleness and last, but by no means least, his behaviour to a young girl here, the only child of one of our most respectable boatmen, has made it absolutely impossible for us to keep him any longer at the University.

"I enclose you here a list of his debts, which I will ask you to pay immediately. I also feel that your bounden duty is to see that he marries Lucy Carr, but I rather think that her father will see to that. I can assure you I feel all the greater pain in sending you this letter at the present moment, just when your eldest son, Adrian Trent, has won such brilliant honours in the schools. He is the first man of the year and Balliol cannot make enough of this exceedingly upright and gifted young man, and you may rest well assured that his University will do everythi towards his future. Let the great success of your eldest son help you to bear the terrible disgrace of the younger one.

"With regrets, I remain,
"Yours faithfully,
"EDWARD CRANE,
"Rector of Exeter."

"P.S.—I understand from Carr that he intends to call upon you immediately."

Mrs. Trent shivered all over. She forgot Adrian and his future, she forgot her noble eldest son and his triumphs. Had she time to give her boy a thought at such a moment, it would have been to curse him for what she called his good luck. As to promoting Adrian's career now, nothing was further from her thoughts.

She began feebly to unfold the tradesmen's accounts—they were always big. This time they were immense. But even if she could meet such cruel bills, the fact was nothing to the other and more terrible fact that her boy was expelled and was expected to marry a common girl, the daughter of a boatman.

"Never," she muttered to herself, with clenched hands.

At this moment, the door of the dining-room was opened and Roberts, the exceedingly respectable and neat young footman, announced that a person by name Carr had just arrived from Oxford and wished to see her on a matter of the most urgent moment.

Mrs. Trent had a hard mouth and cold eyes, otherwise she was considered by the world a handsome woman. She sat for some time without noticing what Roberts had said, she then remarked.

"Put the person into the small room off the hall. I shall be with him when convenient."

By this time she had quite forgotten the letter which she had received from the master of Balliol. The visitor, Carr, was most repellent to her. She supposed she must see the man. As to Val marrying beneath him, it was not to be thought of for an instant. She must, of course, pay Carr a trifle, not much, but something. Those wicked girls were always so designing.

Mrs. Trent looked very dignified when she entered the small room in which Carr stood.

He was a small, round, red-faced man. He had not seated himself and when she entered the room, he pushed a chair towards her, as though he, not she, was the real owner of the room.

To her amazement Mrs. Trent found herself obeying him. She sat with her back to the light. She had a sick sort of feeling that this little man might, if she was not careful, get the better of her. The man, unbidden, began to speak.

"Well, ma'am, I happen to know as rector has writ—I about guess you 'as summat to say."

"I never heard of you before," said Mrs. Trent.

The man laughed—his laughter was exceedingly harsh and loud.

"What?" he cried. "What? You don't mean to deny that you 'as got a letter from rector about my daughter and your lad?"

Mrs. Trent had never quite told a downright lie, but she was getting very close to one now.

She said after another long pause:

"I presume you must be alluding to a little flirtation between your daughter—really girls ought to be more careful—and my son, Adrian."

The man stared, then he burst into a huge laugh.

"I think you are gassin' it a bit, ma'am. I wishes from the bottom o' my heart, as it war a straight chap like Mr. Adrian. Hevery one in Oxford knows about Mr. Hadrian—but it 'as nothing to do with 'im—'e's straight, 'e is— 'e's clever, 'e's gone and covered 'isself with the biggest honours old Balliol can give him. There isn't a man in Oxford, nor a woman neither, that don't love Mr. Adrian, and ma'am you 'ave my 'eartiest congratulations for being the mother of a man like that. No, it ain't Mr. Adrian, bless 'im—but it's 'tother—'im they calls Valentine. And ef you likes to call it a flirtation atween him and my pretty Lucy, I say *no*—there ain't no flirtation between him and my child. She is the only one I have and my wife, she's dead. What I ses, I means—I don't like 'im. No, not one little bit, but he's got to make her an honest woman before the babby comes—that's what I'm arter. 'E's been and done for my Lucy and halthough I fairly 'ates the chap, he 'ave got to marry my gel and set her right with God and the world— and immejit too, so that the poor, innercent bit of an unborn babe 'll have no slur on it, be it boy or girl. You know all about this, ma'am. You have got to help me through with this 'ere marriage."

The little red-faced man stopped talking,

but his eyes were fixed on the woman's white face.

"What you ask is impossible," she said. "You have got to prove your story and so has your daughter. As a matter of fact, I have other views for my son, and a daughter of your's would in no way be a match for Mr. Trent, but admitting *her* indiscretion, I am willing to give her—if the thing is proved—one hundred pounds to remove her from the country."

Carr stared for a minute with his keen black eyes, then his red face became almost purple. He looked round the beautifully furnished room, he thought of his girl and recalled her as she used to be with eyes as blue as the turquoise, with golden fair hair, with such a ringing, merry laugh, with a face all smiles and dimples, and she was his—his only one. He had been intensely proud of her. He had fully intended to do well for her. He had trusted her absolutely and then she had come to him in her bitter, bitter shame and told him the truth. It was one of the undergraduates. It was Mr. Valentine Trent, of Exeter—she supposed her father would turn her out. "I'm a bit stunned," was his answer, "but there's no turning out for you, my gel. Only I tell you what. I'll see you safely married to that young warmint who I 'ates like pison—and who I'd much like to kill—before ever your babe sees the light."

The girl was only half comforted. She scarcely believed it possible that Valentine would make her an honest woman. She went to the little boat-house and sat down to think; her time was not far off. She thought first of all of Val, whom in a sort of way she loved, and then she thought of her father and the flash in his eyes, but even she had no idea of the strength and determination of Carr's will and character. It was owing to Carr that Valentine Trent was being expelled from Oxford, for the troubled and desperate man had gone straight, hot-foot to the rector and with passion in his eyes and anger trembling round his lips, had told the whole horrible story, and the rector, being a father himself, had sympathised with the broken-down man and had advised him to go immediately to see Mrs. Trent at Trent Lodge.

It was finally decided at Exeter, that what with this and the debts—the gambling and the racing, Valentine Trent was no longer fit to be a member of Exeter College.

CHAPTER XX

CARR came a little closer to Mrs. Trent. She had wondered at his long stillness. She was even beginning to think that perhaps she had offered too much money for this stupid little affair. Fifty pounds would doubtless have been sufficient, but then, when she thought these thoughts, she did not know her man. Finding that he approached her slowly and silently, almost like a panther, she spoke again.

" Of course, you must understand, Mr. Carr, that I require absolute proof. At the present moment I have none whatsoever but your word."

" And the rector's," interrupted Carr. " He wrote to ye, ma'am. He's a man of his word, and he told me so."

" Oh, that," interrupted Mrs. Trent, " that letter is a mere nothing. The Rector of Exeter wrote because, in all probability, you, you wicked man, brought him a faked-up story. However—don't come any closer, pray—" she felt the man's breath almost against her cheek "—we will suppose that the whole thing is true, in which case, after sufficient proof, I propose to give you one hundred pounds for your daughter. That sum will take her to Canada, where she will soon pick up a husband in her own class of life. I assure you, my good man, beyond that sum, I intend to do nothing whatsoever."

"Indeed, ma'am, indeed. Now its my turn to speak. I don't want your money—your cursed money. You mayn't believe me, but I wouldn't touch one farthing of it. My pretty Lucy is the only one left to me in life—the only one—the only one, and your wretched, indolent, good-for-nothing son tempted and ruined her—how, God knows, for she has a pure heart, has my Lucy. I want her, for the sake of the unborn child, to become that man's wife, and at once, and I tell you what it is, Mrs. Trent, they must be married in church—nothing else on God's earth will satisfy me, and the marriage must take place at once, because the time of birth is near. Now you know what I've come about. Valentine, that idle scamp, marries Lucy by special licence next week. They can be married quietly at Oxford. She's fifty thousand times too good for him, but he's the father of her child. I'll find him quick enough, and bring him to the scratch—I'm not one to be trifled with. Good-day to you, Mrs.

Trent. It come over me that you'd like to know the best and the worst. A bad man is getting a good, lovely girl to wife and—well, my heart is broken!"

The little round, red-faced man turned and left the room. No one showed him out. He got away by himself. He felt partly stunned, but at the same time his determination was like iron; Valentine Trent should marry Lucy Carr.

He hummed a lively tune under his breath and walked quickly to the railway station.

Mrs. Trent sat for a few minutes after Carr had left her, feeling considerably stunned, then gathering herself well together, she went to her morning room.

The servants had noticed the shabby, black-eyed man. The servants had listened to his loud, emphatic words. Roberts, the young footman, had even gone to the length of eavesdropping a little. What he had overheard had caused him to chuckle, for none of the servants could abide Mr. Val, whereas they all adored Mr. Adrian.

By and bye there came a tap at Mrs. Trent's morning-room and the upper-housemaid entered. She asked if both the young gentlemen's bedrooms were to be got ready that evening.

Mrs. Trent had been in a state of semi-stupor—now she roused herself and said:

"Yes, Hannah, have both rooms got ready, and that reminds me. I want a telegram sent off immediately. Tell Roberts to come for it in five minutes time."

The woman slowly withdrew. Mrs. Trent was now all action. She seated herself by her writing-table, got a telegraph form and filled it in to Adrian Trent at the address of the master of Balliol. She wrote as follows:

"Want you home immediately. Take next train and bring Val with you.

"Mother."

This brief message was received by Adrian Trent shortly after twelve o'clock that same day. He was in the master's study and showed it to him at once.

"I must go, master," he said. "You understand of course that it is absolutely necessary for me to do what I can for my mother."

"Certainly, my dear lad," replied the master, "only whatever happens, Adrian, be firm with regard to that City business. You are absolutely unsuited to the life and the life is unsuited to you. Remember, my dear lad, that this is a matter which will affect your entire future. If your mother is a reasonable woman, and I am sure she must be, she will see the force of your remarks. If it would help you at all, Adrian boy, I would go with you with pleasure to Trent Lodge."

" You are too kind, master, but perhaps I'd best go alone. I want you to understand, sir, that I—I love my mother."

A minute or two later Adrian went away. His first business was to search for Valentine, but he was nowhere to be seen. Then the horrible news was broken to him that his brother was expelled. It was the talk of Exeter and several men spoke of it; his brother must never return to that dearly-beloved home of all learning.

Adrian was terribly stunned, shocked and even a little sick. He felt now that he surely understood his mother. How glad he was that he had not acceded to the master's request. His poor mother—at last—at last she wanted him to comfort her. Adrian felt a glow at his heart as he thought of this.

" Poor dear mater—she knows only too well that there is nothing I would not do for her," was his thought.

He had a few necessary preparations to make before leaving Oxford and in consequence did not get to Winchester until quite late in the day. As he was leaving he had a regular ovation. All the dons of his college came to see their most distinguished young scholar off. The master's last words were:

"I'll see you back again, Trent, in a couple of days."

Little did either of them know.

Mrs. Trent began wandering about her house, putting things to rights, as she expressed it. She was too restless to remain quiet. In particular she wanted to attend to Valentine's comforts. She picked great bunches of sweet peas for his bedroom, she arranged further with the cook that her darling's favourite dishes should be on the table for dinner.

Thus occupied she tried hard to push Carr from her mind. Valentine, when at home, always occupied a large and spacious bedroom. This room faced south. It had three windows and had a door opening into his own special bathroom. Adrian's room was a flight higher up and faced north. The servants did their best to make it comfortable—the mother did not even look at it. When, as she considered, everything was done which could be done for the comfort of her darling, she went into the garden to pick some heliotrope, sweet-smelling geranium and sweet-briar.

Valentine adored sweet scents.

She began to wonder when the boys would arrive. She stood for a moment near the shrubbery, which sheltered one side of the great garden with its well-swept lawns and beds full of roses in the richest bloom. She was suddenly startled by a touch on the shoulder. She turned instinctively and saw Valentine— Valentine, her best beloved, but what—what was wrong? He was changed past recognition, his clothes were torn and shabby, his weak, blue eyes were bloodshot—he was shaking from head to foot.

"Mother," he said in a hoarse whisper.

"Yes, my boy? Come into the house at once, my darling."

"No, mother, only you must see me. Listen —this is life or death. Give me two hundred pounds, mother, and let me go. The money must be in gold, if you can manage it. Notes are useless to me, for they are all marked. I want gold. How much have you got in the house?"

"Nothing approaching that sum, Val. Oh, Val, oh, Val——"

"For God's sake, don't mumble now, mother. Listen, you have got to be very quick. Are the servants at dinner?"

"I expect so. This is their dinner hour."

"I guessed as much," said Val, with a hoarse laugh. "Mater, I can't go into the house. No one must see me. I have a disguise handy which I'll put on in a minute. You go straight to Winchester to the bank, mother, and get me the needful. Ask no questions for heaven's sake, but go, go!"

There was something terrible in the man's face, something beyond all power of expression in the clamouring entreaty of his eyes.

The mother with the force of this one great love of her life walked immediately to Winchester. It was a mile away and the day was a hot one. She did not notice that she was wearing no gloves, that she was altogether in her indoor dress—she, who was as a rule so stately and grand. She panted and puffed as she walked. When she thought the road was clear she even ran a little. By and bye she reached the bank. She secured the necessary money and toiled home.

She went immediately into the shrubbery. A bent old man was sitting smoking under a tree. His beard was snowy white, his clothes very torn and ragged. She started back in terror, but a hand she knew only too well was stretched out to her and she saw at once that this was her son's disguise.

" Have you got it?" he said in a low voice.

" Yes, it is here, all in gold."

" Drop it into my pockets, mother. I can't touch you, for I should soil your white hands;

that's it, mother—that's it, mater. Now good-bye, for ever, and for ever."

" Val, will you tell me nothing ? "

" There's nothing to tell. For God's sake let me get off—good-bye."

He was just leaving the wood, stooping like a very old man, with all the appearance and age of an old man, shabbily dressed, his trousers turned up, his shoes down at heel, when suddenly two smart-looking men, with the brisk air of knowing exactly what they wanted, entered the wood. They bowed very distantly to Mrs. Trent, then each man laid a hand on the bent shoulders of Valentine Trent.

With a swift and instantaneous movement, one man pulled off the wig, the other the false beard and moustaches.

" Ah, Mr. Valentine Trent," said the first. " I thought as much. We hold a warrant for your arrest, sir. It is our duty to arrest you on this warrant. You are charged with the murder of Lucy Carr. Anything that you say now will be taken down as evidence against you. Our orders are to take you back to Oxford and it will be necessary for us to handcuff you. By the way, has the lady been giving you money We are sorry for you, madam, but duty is duty."

The men began to feel in the shabby pockets and waistcoat of Valentine's disguise.

They pulled the disguise off and he stood before them, trembling like the guilty thing he was—he did not attempt to utter a word. He did not even glance at his mother.

The detectives laid the two hundred pounds in a little pile in a handkerchief on the grass.

"I am sorry for you, ma'm," said the first man, "but he won't want any of them where he's going. Come along at once, sir. We've a dogcart waiting outside the gates and we'll just catch our train if we are quick. This is a very nasty business, for there is no doubt about the crime. The body was found early this morning along by the towing-path. We may as well say we had our eyes on you for some little time, sir, and watched you taking her out late last night—the prettiest young gel on the river by a long chalk. Come, sir."

Steel handcuffs were fastened on the young man's wrists and he was taken away from his mother. She stared stupidly at the heap of gold, then she stooped and carefully folding the handkerchief with the gold inside re-entered the house. She went at once to her private sitting-room and put the gold with a jingling noise into an open drawer in her secretaire; then she tumbled as far as the sofa and went off into a heavy swoon.

It was a long time before Mrs. Trent recovered. When she opened her eyes again, she felt exceedingly weak, also very weary and bewildered. For quite ten minutes she couldn't recall what had occurred; then memory fully returned to her and she shook all over, but she was a strong woman—strong physically and strong also in self-control. She rang the bell which brought Roberts upon the scene.

"Roberts," she said in her usual voice, "have the young gentlemen come yet?"

"No madam," replied Roberts. "Me and Hilda, ma'am, we looked up the trains and beggin' your pardon, they can't be here now at the soonest before five-thirty."

"Thank you, Roberts, that will do. Bring me a little tea here and bread and butter. Make the tea strong. I may go up to my room afterwards. If so, tell Hannah that I shall not require her attendance until it is time to dress for dinner. Dinner is to be at eight o'clock. Hannah had better come to me, therefore, at half-past seven, and be sure you let me know when the young gentlemen come."

"Yes, madam, I certainly will, madam."

Roberts faithfully fulfilled his mistress's orders, for no servant dared to disobey Mrs. Trent. The strong tea refreshed her, but she could not manage the bread and butter. She put it adroitly behind some pieces of carved oak in a corner of the room. She would bury it later on. It would never do for the servants to see she was off her appetite. Then, with her usual stately tread she went up to her room and waited.

Nothing mattered to her any more for ever. Her favourite, her idol was arrested and even now locked up on a charge of murder. Yes, murder. He might be hanged! If such an awful catastrophe happened Mrs. Trent was sure she wou'd lose her reason. Why had Val been so mad? Why had he not consulted with her, his mother? But he would never come back any more. He had said good-bye both to her and to life in that awful wood.

She felt not the smallest pang of pity for the murdered girl—all her sorrow was for Valentine. Poor woman, she could have wept her very heart out, but she did not dare even to shed one tear. It was certainly true that Adrian was coming back—Adrian—her eldest son, his head crowned with all the lustre of his young glory, but she hated the glory almost as much as she hated the man.

Her nature was too low down intellectually to grasp his greatness—her nature was too low down morally to perceive his nobility. Her affections had never been his. It is true he had given her love, but she had never returned it, she never would return it now.

Shortly after five o'clock, she listened impatiently for the sound of the motor car, but she could not hear it. Was Adrian, too, going to forsake her?

She rose and began to pace the room with impatience.

" Yes, Hannah, come in," said Mrs. Trent in a tranquil voice.

" The young gentlemen did not arrive by the five-thirty train, ma'am, and the next is at seven."

" Very well, Hannah; some trivial thing has kept them of course. We'd best have dinner at a quarter past eight. Go at once and tell cook."

Hannah disappeared.

At about twenty past seven Adrian Trent arrived alone. He immediately asked for his mother and was told by Roberts in a cheerful, delighted voice that she was in her room dressing for dinner.

" That's all right, Roberts," replied Adrian. " Kindly let my mother know that I am going at once to dress for dinner and will meet her in the drawing-room at eight o'clock."

" Dinner was postponed, Mr. Adrian, until a quarter past," said Roberts.

" That's all right. You might send a cup

Q

of tea to my room. I will explain Mr. Valentine's absence when I see Mrs. Trent."

Adrian had as a rule the bounding step of a very strong young man, but now he went up to the old north room slowly and wearily; he almost felt as though his heart would stop beating.

At the very last moment he had been delayed in Oxford by the frightful tidings of the murder of Lucy Carr. The earlier train had been just moving out of the station when a man had rushed up and pulled him out. There was the strongest suspicion, amounting almost to positive proof of his brother Valentine's guilt in the matter.

As Adrian slowly and quietly dressed he wondered much how he could break the awful shock which he had sustained to his mother. He, of course, knew nothing as yet of the arrest of Valentine. He therefore resolved, come what might, to keep his mother in ignorance of everything until dinner was a thing of the past—then he would tell her the truth. He would try to comfort her—he would endeavour to compass her with his own strong and fervent love. They met, this mother and this young son, in the beautifully furnished drawing-room. The silvery chimes of a little clock, for which Mrs. Trent had given a fancy price, struck one quarter past eight.

Adrian kissed his mother. She returned his caress with the offering of a very icy cold cheek. She was not glad to see him—she had forgotten all about his honours, she took no interest whatsoever in his future.

Adrian had the power of reading thought and her's towards him now was like an open book. He had lived through a bitter time of boyhood and early youth, when he had endeavoured with all his young might to forget his mother's strange want of love for him. The curious thing about the youth was that in spite of her coldness he loved her. He never forgot some words that his father once said to him.

" Adrian, your mother is difficult, but you'll do your best, my boy, to love her for my sake."

As soon as dinner had come to an end Adrian spoke quickly. He began at once by explaining Valentine's absence.

" By the way, mater, on receiving your wire, I would have come by an earlier train, but Val—" he choked a trifle—" Val was occupied. I trust he may come along to-morrow morning. Anyhow I couldn't fail you, mother dear."

"I particularly asked you to bring Valentine," said Mrs. Trent.

" I know—but—but, he wouldn't come So there's an end to that."

For a full minute Mrs Trent was absolutely silent.

"You think he'll come to-morrow," she said at last.

"I sincerely hope so."

"Valentine is the sort of young man who requires most careful management," said Mrs. Trent. "He is remarkably nice-looking and he has a great deal of personal fascination, but harsh words drive such a nature into mischief. You, Adrian, are so terribly goody-goody."

Adrian made no comment. He was well accustomed to his mother's sneers and her unnatural affection for her youngest, worthless son. But he was not angry now, for he loved her as Valentine never could love her and was too full of pity for the awful blow which he must inflict.

"By the way, Adrian, you'd like to have a smoke, and there is of course plenty of whisky and wine."

"I don't want to smoke or drink, mother. I'll have a cup of coffee with you in this room."

"As you please. Roberts, bring in two cups of coffee."

Roberts left the room. He quickly returned with the coffee. Immediately Mrs. Trent poured herself out a cup which by a great effort she forced herself to drink. Adrian did likewise. He never forgot that coffee as long as he lived.

The man, Roberts, came in again to remove the massive silver coffee-service. Suddenly Adrian spoke to him. He went to the door and said in a low tone:

"I shall be engaged with my mother for a time. Do not disturb us."

The man bowed. Adrian turned the key in the lock in such a manner that no one could eavesdrop through the keyhole, then he came back and stood facing his mother. At that moment he looked most truly a glorious specimen of England's gifted youth and brilliant beauty. The fine pose of his head, the square set of his shoulders, the whole expression on the man's face was one to make the heart of any mother to leap in her breast with joy. But alas, this mother was thinking of an old man, sitting against a tree in the shrubbery, and she had no eyes and no glamour for the perfect youth by her side.

After standing and looking at her for a moment Adrian suddenly put his hand on her arm.

She shrank away from him in a sort of terror.

"Don't touch me. I can't bear it!"

"Dearest mother," he said. He was not offended. He remained silent for a minute while his dark grey eyes looked deeply into her. "Do you know?" he said at last in a whisper.

"Yes, God help me, I know. You might have saved him if you would."

"He may have escaped by now, mother. I happen to know he had some money, for I gave him some yesterday. He may be far away now—and safe."

"Then you really don't know, Adrian?"

A sudden unexpected wave of softening flowed over her.

"You do not really know the worst! Your brother, my darling, came here, but only to the shrubbery. Luckily I was out and I saw him. He told me he had committed a crime. He said he wanted two hundred pounds at once. The servants were all at dinner, I got it for him from our bank. Oh, my beautiful boy! When I came back I found him disguised as an old man. Nobody would know him. I stuffed his pockets with gold. He was just about to leave me when two of those brutal detectives came up and—Adrian—they arrested my son! My son—on the charge of murder! Adrian, as I look now into your eyes, I think, notwithstanding the fact that I always loved Valentine best, yet that you, Adrian, you, for some extraordinary reason, love me best."

CHAPTER XXI

"Little mother, that is true," said Adrian Trent. "My mother, that is indeed true."

"Prove it, Adrian, by saving him."

"I?" said Adrian, aghast and stricken. "I—forgive me—I don't know what you mean! How am I to save him?"

Mrs. Trent stood up. She laid her hand now with great emphasis on Adrian's arm. "I leave the matter to you. You have talent—you can contrive. I am worn out by grief. Win my love by saving Valentine—no matter how!"

The young man looked at her with absolute horror on his face. She turned and left him. Just as she reached the door, she turned and came back a few steps.

"Remember, if Valentine is convicted, I shall go mad—raving mad. Use your wits to good purpose. You are clever, you can think of something. Good-night."

As long as he lived Adrian Trent never forgot that awful night. Sleep indeed was far from him. He went to his bedroom, but he did not go to bed. His whole brain was consumed with anxious thought. If Valentine, who was worthless, who was sent down, who had murdered the prettiest girl who had ever talked to the young undergrads, the girl who was so young, whose eyes were like two bits of the sky at their bluest, and whose hair was thick and long and golden, if he was openly convicted of this murder, Adrian's own mother would lose her senses.

It seemed to Adrian that he saw even now the first gleam of that madness in her fierce eyes. She loved Val—she had never cared for him. The want of her love had been the great miss in his life, for he was only a little fellow when his manly father left him. From that moment the strange thing was that while Val treated his mother with a sort of affectionate, easy contempt, which only meant coaxing and petting when he wished for money, and total indifference the rest of the time, Adrian honestly and fervently loved her.

At the time of his great triumph, most of the other men had mothers and sisters who clung to them and admired them, but he was alone. It is true the master and the dons and the men of his year crowded round to congratulate him, but the face he wished for of all others was not present, the love he wished for above all other loves was not forthcoming in his hour of triumph.

He sat through the weary hours of that summer night in his dingy, cheerless bedroom. As the early morning broke, he sat down and wrote a brief note.

"Mater, you had best burn this immediately after reading it. I could not mistake your words of last night, and all I ask you in return for that which I have made up my mind to do is to love me—a little. I will give you back Valentine in my own way at my own time, but I shall never probably see you again. Only, mother, it would in a degree comfort me to take with me to the hour of trial—to the convict cell— in all probability to the hangman's rope, the love of my mother. I do this thing—this very great thing—for you. I give up all my future—and, mother, it could be magnificent and glorious—but I cast away the honours— how worthless they are after all—and the possibility of great work in the world— entirely for you. Think of me with tenderness by and bye. Love me a little in return—that is, if you can.

"ADRIAN."

This note Adrian carefully addressed, carefully sealed with his father's seal, then he marked it private and then he himself pushed under his mother's door.

Thus, after she awoke, Hannah brought her the note with her early cup of tea. The woman read the contents of this letter with blazing eyes and quivering lips, then she muttered rapidly under her breath:

"Poor boy! Poor, dear boy. No, no, it shall not be. He is so quixotic, just like his father. That is going too far. No, I never quite meant that. I didn't mean him to give his life for me. No, as there is a God above, I did not mean that. I will stop him. I must stop him."

There was a bell close to her bedside. She rang it violently. Hannah, in some wonder, appeared.

"Hannah," said Mrs. Trent. "Find Mr. Adrian immediately. I wish to speak to him at once before I dress."

"Mr. Adrian, madam? He left the house quite three hours ago."

"Oh," said Mrs. Trent. "You can leave me now, Hannah."

The woman obeyed. Mrs. Trent was at first terribly puzzled what to do. That flush of admiration whith had risen in her breast with regard to her splendid son had suddenly faded. Had Adrian remained at home she was certain she would have tried to divert him from his purpose. But he was away—she could not tell where. He had therefore given her no choice.

It was unfair to put her into such a predicament. She read the letter over again more calmly, then, noticing Adrian's command at the beginning of his epistle—' Burn this letter '—she got tremblingly out of bed, lit a candle and carefully and slowly consumed it. She then felt freer and to a certain extent happier. There was nothing whatever for her to do but to sit still and await events.

Of course Adrian would not be so mad as to throw away his life. She might of course go to Oxford and see the master of Balliol, but no, she must on no account do that, for it would tell against Valentine.

Adrian was going to accomplish the supreme sacrifice and all he asked in return from her was a little love. She tried very hard to arouse that feeling in her breast, but endeavour as she might, it would not come.

Meanwhile Adrian went quickly back to Oxford. Two or three old friends saw him and greeted him with respect which all men show to an overmastering sorrow, for the news of Valentine's being sent down and also of his immediate arrest on a charge of murder had spread like wildfire through the city.

Adrian took hardly any notice of those with whom he had been so warmly affectionate. People remarked afterwards that he looked very white and haggard. He went straight to the boat house on the Isis. There were the boats—quite a hundred of them—drawn up in rows, just outside the picturesque little dwelling. How proud blue-eyed Lucy had been of the pretty flowers which were blooming everywhere, how proud she was of the tea-garden where she had served teas to so many of the undergrads.

Many girls were prime favourites on the river, but there was no one like Lucy—no one so tall, straight and beautiful, no one so much beloved. Adrian now stooped his tall head and entered the house. As a matter of fact he had never been there before, but his quick observant eyes saw many signs of a woman's dainty skill. There was a basket with some knitting, a work-box wide open—there was a little silver thimble with turquoise rim and close to the thimble was a case of scissors of different sizes—all embellished with the pretty turquoise stone.

The fire was out on the hearth, although the day, for the time of the year, happened to be a cold one. A man, who looked old and bent, was seated in a wicker chair by the empty grate, his brawny arms were hanging helpless by his side, his head was bent forward and was lying against his breast. There was something about this man's attitude, which roused Adrian to a wild passion of anger. He approached him slowly.

"Carr, old chap, don't take on. I've come to speak to you."

Carr raised his sunken and blurred eyes. He looked full at Adrian.

"You go out," he said, "I don't want your sort about. She's stone dead, my pretty one—my little Lucy, my golden flower—and he, thank the good Lord, he's safe in gaol. They had him before the magistrates this morning, and he's to take his trial in about a week. You 'as a look of him now I come to see you more closely. Well, now, to be sure, if you ain't the young swell what has gone and took all the honours. The Varsity war proud o' ye, but I rayther somehow guess it won't be so proud o' ye in the future. Ye are—young fellow—own brother to a murderer. That ain't illuminating, that ain't, eh? Or if it be, it is the wrong way round. Honours for you one minute, disgrace, black and shameful, the next. Look ye here, young chap, I mean to do for that brother o' yours—he shall hang by the neck, as sure as my name is Josiah Carr. He'll hang, that's it—hang! And I'll scream with joy on the day his neck is broke. Now, you look here, young man, what have you come bothering me for?"

"I wish to ask you a few questions," said Adrian.

"Ask away—I don't care. There's naught on airth will save him from his fate."

"Would it be possible for me to see her, your little flower?"

"See her? No. The crowner has got the body and the whole city is subscribing for a grand funeral."

"Mr. Carr—I wouldn't have come—if I didn't pity you."

"And I hates your pity—bah! it gives me nausea."

"Well," said Adrian, after a pause. "I won't speak of it, but may I ask you a question or two?"

"Ef your questions don't go in favour of the prisoner."

"I think I can assure you on that point."

"Werry well. Speak and be quick."

"Where did she die, Mr. Carr? And how did she die?"

"Man, do you want to tear my wounds open afresh? Lucy, she come and she told me the truth. She was a bit frightened like—but she tell't her old dad all and him and his honeyed words and all. And I said, 'He'll marry you and make an honest woman o' you, little gel, and God forgive me, I went out o' the house when I never ought to have stirred. All night I walked and walked and walked and when the day broke I took train to Winchester and I seed his grand mother. I 'ad my spin out with her. I talked straight to the pint. Then I come home. I can't say what happened in my absence. It was getting on late—I wondered the place didn't look more usual —but I guessed there wasn't many wanting boats that day, for the sun had gone in and the clouds were coming up black and cruel. For all that, the flowers were drooping like and the place wasn't rigged up as Lucy was proud to keep it. When I entered this room—walking very strong, sir—the first thing I seed was the back of the golden head and she was seated in that werry chair and I called out hearty as you please, 'Lucy, my gel, its all right,' but she neither spoke nor turned. My heart went down a peg, but not much. I went straight up to her—straight up to her—and took her little lily-white hand and then—God in heaven above —it seemed as though I turned mad on the spot! Her blue eyes were wide open, but she didn't see me and she war cold as marble. Her dress war all wet, but I tore it open and there was a little hole, not a big 'un, mind you, but jest a tiny one under the left breast, and there was a queer-shaped dagger lying on the floor. Never seen that sort o' thing afore. I went like a madman for the police and two o' their werry best detectives motored out as fast as they could to his mother's place and took the scoundrel in cold blood. And now he's to serve his trial—and—and—don't ask me any more, sir."

" Would you mind showing me the dagger ? "

" No—no—I couldn't and I wouldn't. Its kept as evidence against him—the black-hearted scoundrel."

Adrian slowly left the house and walked down the towing-path. He was anxiously making his own plans. On the day before he left Oxford Valentine had come to him and had begged most earnestly—even passionately—for the loan of sixty or seventy pounds.

" You're so rich, you can well afford it, Adrian," he had said.

" I'll let you have it of course," said Adrian. " But I wish you wouldn't worry the mother with so many debts."

" Oh, I won't worry her. Thanks old chap. The luck is all your way. You have the money and all. I suppose, by the way we both go home to-morrow."

"You do," said Adrian. "The master has very kindly asked me to stay with him for a few days."

"And you will stay, old man?"

Valentine's eyes glittered eagerly.

"Yes, I shall stay."

"Well," Val had continued, pocketing his cheque, "as I remarked before, the luck is all on your side—damnation on mine, but I mean to have a merry night before I leave the dear old place. I've invited a lot of fellows to my rooms—we are getting up a bit of a row—nothing wrong of course, but I'm in it. By the way, do you remember that curious Italian dagger you brought some years ago now from Italy?"

"Of course. I am rather proud of my dagger. I bought it in a queer shop in a back street in Naples and the man told me, the tip—just the mere tip—was poisoned. The hilt is very beautifully carved, and I think of giving it to the master before I leave. He is fond of curios."

"Lend it to me, Ad, old man, like a good chap. I have talked of your wonderful dagger to so many friends of mine and they are all devoured with curiosity to have a look at it. You may as well let me take it. I'll bring it back to you to-morrow before I start for home."

Adrian had been unwilling.

"I ought not to lend it to you," he said. "If you and your boon companions get excited, you may prick each other with the point of the dagger and the slightest prick is death."

Valentine had laughed.

"I'll be careful, old man, never you fear. I want to frighten two or three with it, that's all. You'll see it back early to-morrow morning. Ah, there it is, hanging on your wall. Lucky for me! So-long for the present."

* * * * * * *

When Mrs. Trent found herself deprived of both of her sons she quickly made up her mind. She determined to read no newspapers of any sort whatsoever and to listen to no gossip. She would live alone in her lonely world. She sometimes had moods of silence when all her servants were afraid of her. She had one on now—one deep and terrible. She never left her room. The only person she saw was Hannah and she desired Hannah not to speak to her and not to bring her any letters, telegrams or newspapers. There was a great deal of talk in the servants' hall, but in the mistress's bedroom there was profound silence.

Mrs. Trent ate her food, she took a strong opiate every night. She looked terribly old—she looked haggard to the last degree, but she kept her feelings to herself.

The servants knew a great deal of what was going on and the mistress knew that they knew, but not for the world would she question them. She felt quite certain that the end would come some time or other before long. One boy would be taken—the other left. Which, O God, which?

About three weeks after Adrian had written to his mother the door of her bedroom was quietly opened and Valentine entered. His face was something fearful to behold. It was white as death itself—his eyes were sunk in his head.

"I've come back," he said.

"Then you are saved—you are acquitted, my boy," she faltered.

"My God! At such a price," said Valentine. "The noblest fellow on God's earth saved me. He took it on his own shoulders—every bit of it. It was the dagger did the business—otherwise he could not have got the judge and the jury to believe him. I was at the last gasp in the prisoner's dock when he came in. He looked very white and splendid. He couldn't have managed it so neatly—but that old Carr was dead. And Carr must have burnt my letters to poor Lucy. Carr was found dead in the very chair where they put Lucy after I stabbed her with the dagger.

"They will hang Adrian. I waited to hear the result. Now, don't mention his name to me again. Upon my soul, I wouldn't have let him do it only for the horrible thought of the hangman's rope. Think what he has done for me. Never speak to me about him, mother—and, mother, you could have prevented it—and I hate you, mother, for letting him do it. I've come back to you, for what I'm worth, but I hate you."

If there were two unhappy people in this world it was Mrs. Trent and her son, Valentine. Adrian's sentence had been commuted to imprisonment for life and his marvellous escape from Hartleypool prison and his meeting with Elizabeth have already been told. But Val, who grew worse and weaker, as the days, weeks and months passed over his head, could bear his anguish no longer.

One day he managed to get into Winchester. He saw a doctor who told him that both heart and lungs were seriously affected and that he had but a short time to live. He gave a kind of sob which puzzled the clever doctor, but there and then he went straight to the telegraph office and sent off the telegram to Captain Marshall demanding his instant attendance and declaring his guilt.

There never was a man more staggered than

the governor of the great prison when he received the telegram. He turned round, looked at Elizabeth, great tears filled his eyes, he put the little flimsy sheet of paper into her hands. She read it with a strange, triumphant smile.

"I always, always knew it," she said, "although I did not know the particulars. He wanted to tell me but I would not let him."

"Miss Beaufort," said the governor, "write a line at once to your mother to say you will be away, perhaps for two or three days, and then come with me We will both together visit Valentine Trent and together we will receive his hideous confession."

CHAPTER XXII

Elizabeth sat down in her studio and wrote a hurried line to her mother. She was trembling exceedingly. The anguish of the last hour had kept her calm, but the sudden and most unexpected deliverance knocked her down utterly. She wrote with the hand of an old woman, not with the bold signature for which she was famous. The letter, however, was written and Elizabeth and the governor of Hartleypool prison drove swiftly into Hartleypool where it was posted.

Various people saw them as they passed and great and abounding was their amazement. Mrs. Heavyfoot in particular stood with arms akimbo and a smile on her crafty face.

"Ha! ha!" she said to a neighbour. "I knows what I knows. Miss is gettin' it 'ot—'ot! Ain't she with the governor himself?"

A woman, a gentle-faced woman laughed in her face.

"Whatever do yer mean?" she inquired. "'Ow is our Miss Elizabeth gettin' it 'ot?" she asked.

"Lor blesh yer, Liza, ain't she with the governor?"

"Well, and what o' that?"

"What o' that, my good woman, you wait and see. I tell ye, there'll soon be news—beautiful, refreshin' news!"

"I don't see it," said the woman. "If our Miss Elizabeth chooses to drive with the governor I see naught in it unless indeed he's a-courtin' of her. You 'as a sour mind, Mrs. Heavyfoot, and you're mighty fond o' puttin' the cart afore the horse."

"I tell ye, she's wanted," said Mrs. Heavyfoot. "Them as sins is allus wanted. Does yer read yer bible—the wages o' sin, ye knows, the wages o' sin."

"Folly," said the woman. "I wouldn't call it much o' the wages o' sin to see a smart young lydy like our Miss Beaufort talking as friendly as you please to his gracious highness the captain, and the captain smiling at her like anything at all, and no warders about and no handcuffs on. Talk sense when ye can and if ye can't keep silence."

Whereupon Mrs. Heavyfoot thumped into her house and banged the children all round. She certainly could not understand the aspect of affairs. Elizabeth looked positively cheerful. She, that wicked one, looked radiant.

There was a bright colour in her cheeks and although she did not take the least notice of Mrs. Heavyfoot that woman heard her laughter, swift and true.

Then came the next news in the little drama. The captain, bless him, must be goin' a courtin', for he and Miss Elizabeth took a first-class express to London, no less.

Mrs. Heavyfoot wished now most ardently that she had not made an enemy of Elizabeth. She even began to try to undo her evil words.

"Her—Miss, as I calls her—is werry handsome," she said. "A beautiful face, yes. I, meself, in some ways prefers her to Mr. Pat. Mr. Pat is winsome, to be sure, but Miss Elizabeth, she's wunnerful true. Neighbours all, ye couldn't catch her out in a falsehood. No, no, I knows what I knows. I was only wanting to have a bit of a rise out o' ye, neighbours, that's it. When her comes back married to his 'ighness, the captain, her'll do well for Heavyfoot, that I'm sure. She's allus been werry friendly wi' me."

But the neighbours did not think much of Heavyfoot's chances and Heavyfoot himself was sulky and told his wife to shut up. He had learnt the prudence of silence in his employment and he could have electrified those women had he told them what he really knew, that the captain had gone with two warders to the studio and that immediately afterwards a telegraphic form had come for the captain and he, Heavyfoot himself, had brought it to the studio. And the captain, why he had read it and had shown it to Miss Beaufort and his face was all smiles and sunshine and he had told the warders to go home for they were not wanted. Ah, if he could have told *that* news, but he didn't—not to the women with their tongues. ' The tongue of a woman, it is truly awful,' he said to himself.

Meanwhile the governor of the prison and Elizabeth Beaufort went quickly not to London, but to Exeter, where they changed for Winchester, that well known and historic town.

They spoke very little on the journey. Elizabeth was strangely quiet because she felt so strangely, so marvellously glad. They reached Winchester about eight in the evening and took a taxi-cab immediately to Trent Lodge.

As they approached this beautiful and stately home the captain knew well that the girl by his side was trembling exceedingly. He turned and faced her.

"My dear," he said, " you ought not to do that. Think how brave you have been in times of great peril and perplexity. Be brave now for the sake of—for the sake of—need I say it? The man you love."

Then tears came into those great, glorious eyes, and Elizabeth laid her little hand in that of the governor's and whispered in a choking voice.

"It is only the great, the unspeakable relief."

"Yes, my dear, yes. I quite understand. We always break down when things get a bit easier, don't we? But all the same you must keep your courage up."

"I will. I promise," she replied.

Then they reached Trent Lodge and the servant opened the door.

"I have come," said the governor, speaking in his quiet and exceedingly dignified manner, "in reply to a telegram. I am the governor of Hartleypool prison. Is Mr. Valentine Trent still alive?"

"Oh, oh, lor', sir." Poor Roberts fell back with a face like chalk. "He's very bad, sir," he said, after a pause. "I know he 'ave been raving like, but I don't think, not for a minute, that the Missus 'll let you in."

"Go to Mr. Valentine Trent and say that I've come here with a lady."

The man went shaking away. There was no getting over the command in that voice. The governor and Elizabeth waited in the splendid and spacious hall, riches and luxuries everywhere, a vista of sunny rooms, a vista of beautiful pictures, a vista of the loveliness of the earth. Then there came a noise and a scuffle and a woman's piercing cry.

"That is the mother, I presume," said Captain Marshall. "I shall go to him myself."

"Not alone. I'll go with you," said Elizabeth.

"As you like, my dear, as you like."

But before he could say a word further, a tall woman, richly dressed in velvet and magnificent Spanish lace, came out of a certain door accompanied by an emaciated and almost exhausted youth.

"Ha! ha! I said I'd do you yet, mother, and I have. By jove, I have! Mother, you have been a *brute* to your eldest son, and the thing has killed me, yes, killed me. Sir, are you Captain Marshall?"

"I am, young gentleman."

"You'll be taking me back to prison, won't you?"

"That depends—I should like to speak to you. Allow me to introduce Miss Elizabeth Beaufort. She, heaven bless her, looked farther and deeper into the truth than I did, and she was the direct means of saving your noble brother."

"Oh," said Valentine, "oh! God bless you! God bless you!"

The miserable creature grovelled on his knees at the girl's feet.

"Get up, Valentine Trent," she said, in her calm voice. "Mrs. Trent I can tell you a great deal about your eldest and noble son."

"Come this way. Let's hear! let's hear!" said Valentine.

He tottered as he walked. Elizabeth held out her hand to support him. He pushed his mother aside with an oath.

"If you do take him to your prison, you won't keep him long," said Mrs. Trent.

She turned as she spoke and looked at the governor.

"Dear Madam," he replied in his most courteous manner, "I have only come here to-day to get information and this young lady, this noble girl, whom I was about to arrest, supposing that she had harboured a felon in her studio near Hartleypool, I have thought right to bring with me. She can give you great and profound comfort with regard to your eldest son."

They entered a very large room. The sick man flung himself on to a sofa. He bore a strange and fleeting likeness to Adrian—a likeness that came and went. It was extraordinary. It played about his lips and eyes and vanished. He was Adrian deprived of his strength, his nobility. He was Adrian, the coward, the felon, and yet, was he in very truth a coward then?

Mrs. Trent took not the slightest notice of her unwelcome guests, but she put a strong stimulant between her son's lips. He looked up at her with a ghastly smile.

"Out with the truth, mother. You have promised. You know you have promised."

"I—I—oh, Val, my boy, Val! It may be all right yet. Don't—don't force me. Have pity on me, my own, own darling son."

"I have none, and I may as well say at once that I hate you. I'd a thousand times rather have died than gone through what you dragged me through. Oh, when *he* came to the court—my God, when he came into the court—sir, young lady, he had won the highest, the very highest honours that Oxford could bestow upon those she loves. He was covered with glory and he was loved, yes, loved by rich and poor alike. I was a sneak, a gambler—worse, worse—yes, of course, I meant to be, I was. I went wrong with a girl. She had a pretty face; then I got frightened and I stole Adrian's dagger and I stabbed her in the heart. The tip was poisoned, and I knew a prick would do the work. I dragged her home and tried to make my escape. She looked so pretty when she was dead. Upon my soul, I kissed her on her little white face, and since then she has haunted me day and night, always and always and ever and ever I see the face of Lucy Carr—the prettiest girl on the river—and, as there is a God above, I see another face—my brother's! Oh, the horror! Can I forget that scene in court. Now, mother, go on. I'm spent—worn out. Go on!"

"I made Adrian do it," said Mrs. Trent. "I don't mind what I say now. I forced Adrian to do what he did. I suppose it was fine of him, but I could only think of the boy I loved. You see, Captain Marshall, I didn't love Adrian. He was a bit too great for me. He was like his father. His father was great too. But this boy I worshipped, and now he hates me."

"So I do! so I do! oh, my God, where's Adrian? Where's my brother? Did you save him, young lady? Come close, close, and tell me all."

There was a long pause of deep silence. "Not a word," said Elizabeth then—"not a syllable until you recant those cruel words! Before I help you to find your brother you must tell your poor, poor mother that you in very truth give back mistaken love for mistaken love."

" Oh, oh, all right, Madre. Of course, we've always been chums, haven't we ? "

He held out his shaky hand. The woman bent and devoured it with kisses. Then her cold, hard eyes turned and looked at Elizabeth.

" You despise me ? "

" No, poor tormented soul," said the girl and, strange as it may seem, Mrs. Trent, the proud, the distant, fell into the embrace of Elizabeth Beaufort, and gave her heart to her for ever.

CHAPTER XXIII

During his last days on earth Valentine Trent with all the feeble impatience of the very ill and dying, kept Elizabeth Beaufort by his side. She took a kind of control over him which he sadly wanted. She insisted on his going to bed and then helped his mother to nurse him, but the miserable creature turned away from his mother, frowning and fretting whenever she entered the room.

This conduct made the poor broken-down lady so unhappy that at last Elizabeth begged to be allowed to sit alone with him for a short time. It was not that in any manner she liked him, how could she like one so mean and worthless? But her heart was very big, her affection very deep. If Adrian Trent could endure this man and allow himself to be falsely accused and imprisoned for his sake, or rather for the sake of their mother, surely she, Elizabeth, was the last woman on earth to shrink from him now?

Nevertheless she knew that the time had arrived when for that mother's sake she must speak to him.

"Valentine," she said, "I don't want you to talk. I want you to listen. You have gone through all the terrible tortures of remorse. You have discovered for yourself that the wages of sin is death. But at last, Valentine, at long last, you have confessed your awful crime, and your confession has been fully written down and duly witnessed. Poor Valentine, your time on earth is very short."

"But—but—I *dread* to die," cried out the miserable man.

"Now, try and keep calm," said Elizabeth. "Please remember that in any case for a crime like yours there is *no* forgiveness except through the door of death. The law of the land will convict you, Valentine, and there will be no mercy shown to one like you. Yet, think, think of the merciful, most merciful God. He allows you to remain in your bed, in your own most comfortable home. He indeed is full of pity. You can cry for that great forgiveness which is never withheld from those who seek it. I tell you, Valentine, the Lord God is mighty to save—and He, who loves all His creatures, will save even you."

"Do you indeed believe it possible?" said the dying man, fixing his mournful eyes on the girl's strong young face.

"I am quite certain about it. He is with

you now and He is mighty to save. He was with you and helped you to make your great confession. If you cling to Him and turn to Him He will be with you till the end—strong to deliver. Yes, Valentine, strong to deliver. But listen, I have one thing I must—I will say."

"Say it—say anything," was the whispered answer.

"Very well, it is this. You like to have me near you. I stay with you, Valentine Trent, for the sake of your noble, your splendid brother."

"Ah, yes. He is all that. I like to hear you talk of him as you do. I have a—a thought in me that perhaps you even love my brother."

Elizabeth looked fully into the weak face.

"I love him with all my heart and soul," she replied.

"I say, that is good hearing. Old Ad will come home and be happy yet when I am under the sod."

"I have something else which I must speak to you about."

"Say it—say it!"

"You like to have me with you."

"My God, I should think I do. You give me the most wonderful courage."

"But Valentine, I cannot remain any longer."

"What? what?" There came a weak scream of anguish.

"I cannot stay any longer for I will not turn your mother out. What she did, she did for you, for you alone, and now you spurn her from you. Your treatment of her is unspeakably cruel. It is worse—it is outrageous. I will not stay to witness it."

"Oh, oh, oh! Then I shall die."

"Die, then! I am going."

The girl rose from her place by the bedside. A fevered hand tried to pull her back.

"I—I—oh, this awful weakness! Suppose I turn and be good to her, will you stay?"

"Valentine, if you love her as she deserves from *you* and from *you alone*, and if in addition you use your influence to get her to see your brother in his true light, on those conditions I will stay."

"To the end? Will you?"

"Yes, to the end."

"Then I'll do it, Elizabeth. Yes, I'll do it. Poor old Madre. Yes, I'll be good."

"And really love her, Valentine. And you will talk to her as I ask you to do about your brother?"

"My God, yes, oh, yes."

"Then I'll fetch her at once and stay away from the room for the present."

Meanwhile the governor of the great prison of Hartleypool had a heavy and most important task before him. There were certain necessary steps to go through immediately and in consequence he put, according to the law, a guard on Trent Lodge, a guard who looked like an ordinary servant, and he sent a well known locum tenens to take his place at the prison. Then with Valentine's written confession in his hand, he went to interview the Home Secretary in order that a full pardon might be granted to a perfectly innocent man. He also went before the Grand Assizes and put the case of his young favourite, Elizabeth Beaufort, so fully and so pathetically before these officers of the State that considerably under a week a full pardon was granted to Adrian Trent, and Elizabeth Beaufort was declared absolutely free.

But now a difficulty arose, for no one knew *where* Adrian Trent had gone. Even Elizabeth did not know although she told what little she did know. As to herself, she had made her promise and would keep it. She remained day in, day out, with the dying man and with his mother, who clung to her, and when, owing to Valentine's intervention, the elder woman began to see her elder son in his true light, the real nobleness and greatness of his character was fully revealed to her.

"And he did it for me—for me!" she sobbed.

Thus those three, one on the border of the grave, one whose tortured heart was broken, one again who was strong and brave, all talked of Adrian, always and forever of Adrian Trent. And Elizabeth was never tired of telling to her anxious listeners how and in what sort of manner she had saved Adrian.

"Oh, but do I not love you," whispered the dying man.

Mrs. Trent with tears streaming from her sunken eyes echoed these words.

"I love you, Elizabeth Beaufort," she said. "It is not in my nature to love many, but I love you."

Thus it came to pass that Valentine, like the thief on the cross, found peace at the long end. Elizabeth happened to be alone with him when he passed on to a land where even black crimes like his are forgotten and forgiven.

He looked at her and smiled, and his smile at the very last was almost what Adrian's might have been.

"I am no longer afraid," he whispered very low to Elizabeth Beaufort. "I want the long, long rest—the long, long peace. Owing to you I feel most certainly that God has forgiven even one so black as myself."

Then he smiled again and looked more like Adrian than ever, and so he passed away.

(ANSI and ISO TEST CHART No 2)

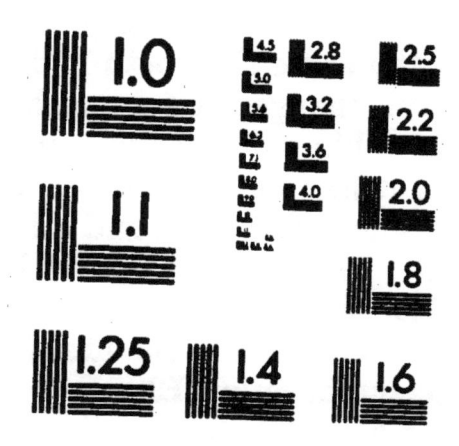

CHAPTER XXIV

Now it so happened that Henry Counsellor did remarkably well in the great city of New York. He kept up the name Elizabeth had given him. He could have changed it for another, but she had given it to him and that was enough.

New York is like no other place, perhaps, in the world. The young man had a little money in his pocket. He was young. He had a noble carriage. He was neatly and respectably dressed. It was essential for him to get on in order that he might return Elizabeth her money. He asked for a post in a great business house, and, strange to say, obtained it.

He did admirably where he was put. He was much liked and, above all things, he was deeply respected. His manner was cheerful and sunny, but he looked like one who would permit no liberties, and no one thought of offering them to him.

He took a suite of rooms in one of the many hotels. He joined a good club. Everyone said Counsellor would rise high in the land of his adoption. His chief could not make enough of him. The very few people he condescended to make friends with thought him the best fellow on earth. As to the others they looked on with envy and longing. But Counsellor had one peculiarity. If there was a neighbour or a friend, or even a stranger, in any difficulty or trouble, then he shewed himself in a new light. He made the case of the unfortunate his own.

As circumstances turned out, he was only a short time in New York, but even during that time he put more than one man, lad and girl upon their feet once more. He said to himself that he did this for the sake of Elizabeth, but he really did it because he could not help himself, because it was his nature.

On a certain evening there was a great dinner at his own special club. It was given in this remarkable young man's honour. He was requested to take the chair, and there were many toasts given on his account. He was fêted and made much of. It is hard to say whether he liked it or not. His grave, steadfast eyes seemed to look through the speakers, as though they would penetrate to their very souls. It was whispered that Counsellor did not like praise.

Then, before he went away, he entered that room in the club where all the papers, both English and American, were set out in neat rows. It was well for him that he happened to be alone at this moment, for his eyes were attracted to the following paragraph:

"*Will a man known in England as Adrian Trent return to that country immediately in order to receive a free pardon from the king for the crime he has never committed. His brother is dead and has confessed all.*
"*Elizabeth Beaufort.*
"*Henry Marshall,
Governor of Hartleypool.*"

Now this extraordinary paragraph looked so very like the truth that on the following day Henry Counsellor cabled to the governor of the prison. All he said was:

"Have seen paragraph. Is it true?"

The governor was now back again at Hartleypool. The cable was to be replied to—not to Adrian Trent, but to a certain number.

"*True as God*," was the governor's response.

Now, indeed, there was no time to lose. Henry Councellor, not saying a word of his true story to his chief, said that important news compelled him to return to England immediately.

"But you will come back again, my good Henry," said the chief.

"Perhaps," said Counsel. His eyes were wonderfully bright.

"I shall miss you, lad. You suit me," said the chief.

"I am sorry, sir. I shall never forget your kindness."

"Well now, let me do something for you," said the chief. "I don't suppose you are over-flush with the coin, and if you are suddenly called to England, you will want—well, to make matters brief—I will pay your passage. The *Lusitania* sails to-morrow."

"I will allow you to do it, my dear sir, if I on my part may make a condition. It is this. May I return to New York *with my wife* and give you back the money, which is at present a great convenience?"

"Ah, I thought there was a girl in the case," was the great millionaire's inward comment. "Agreed, old fellow," he said, aloud, patting the supposed Counsellor on the shoulder. "Upon my word, I shall miss him," thought the millionaire.

Thus and in this manner Counsellor returned to England.

He went immediately back to Hartleypool and saw the governor. It is not too much to say that the governor absolutely wept when he beheld this splendid looking man. He even laid his old grey head on the young man's breast and kissed him.

"Oh, my boy, my boy," he said. "You are as free as the very air, my noble, most noble boy."

"I say, dear governor, I want *her*. Where is she?" Trent's voice trembled and was a trifle muffled in tone.

"All in good time, my lad, all in good time. She's as safe as can be and is waiting for you. But you must give the old man one—one honour."

"Anything, my dear sir."

"I want," said the governor, "to walk through Hartleypool from end to end leaning on your arm, so that every warder in this place and every warder's wife shall know the truth, the whole truth and nothing but the truth. Come, Adrian, this is my little joyful revenge. Immediately afterwards we will go to Elizabeth Beaufort."

Adrian could not help feeling a slight impatience, but the old man was resolute. He gave directions to certain members of his staff, and then he started on his slow walk. He, so old and feeble, the youth by his side so gallant in his bearing. From every cottage in Hartleypool the people came out to see the sight and amongst them, of course, Mrs. Heavyfoot.

She said afterwards that she nearly fell, that she had what is called "a spasm of the 'art."

But the governor was laughing and joking and talking, and the young man was doing likewise.

Some little children ran up and Trent put shillings into their hands to buy sweetmeats, and smiled down at their curly mops of hair, but when they reached Mrs. Heavyfoot's cottage the governor said:

"Walk on alone for a minute, my boy. Go towards the railway station. I am coming with you. I have a word to say to this woman."

Trent could do nothing but obey. He was puzzled at the whole scene. It so happened that Heavyfoot was at home, and stood by his wife's side.

"You recognise that gentleman," said the governor.

"I does so, yer honour."

"Well, I thought I'd just mention to you that he is a free man, that what he did he did in a deep and noble sense of honour. *He* commit murder—not he! It would be much more in *your* walk of life, *Mrs*. Heavyfoot, and now I wish further to add that neither you nor your wife suit me, Heavyfoot, and you will leave to-morrow for an inferior prison and get away from Hartleypool. I don't blame you so much as your wife, but that sort of woman cannot be allowed to make mischief at Hartleypool."

Then the governor stopped at the house of the

gentle-faced young woman who had helped Mrs. Heavyfoot to take care of Lizzie and told her quite simply and frankly that her husband was appointed to Heavyfoot's position.

"Heavyfoot leaves to-morrow," he said, "and our missing convict is the bravest and best man on earth. Three cheers for our *missing convict!* Lads, boys, girls, take up the cry! Three cheers for the man who was not only proved to be innocent, but NOBLE. I mean to give you all a feast in his honour and on that occasion I shall have the pleasure of telling you a certain portion of his true story."

"What are they cheering about?" said Trent.

"Why, about you, lad, you, of course. Now, here's the train. We are just in time. We'll get to your old home, Trent Lodge, to your mother and to Elizabeth Beaufort this ev

"My God, it is too much," said Trent.

It was hard to make a man of his s but tears did dim the splendour of his great eyes.

CHAPTER XXV

THERE are dark times in life, but by no means always dark. There are times when the sun comes out from behind thick banks of cloud, when the birds sing riotously, when the flowers open their sweet petals and there is gladness where there was misery—there is, in short, hope where there was despair.

Such was the case on a sunny evening in the heart of a golden June. A girl all in white, very erect, very stately, with the magical beauty of personality and character all over her, was walking slowly in a well kept garden. A woman much older than herself was keeping pace with her. Now and again the eyes of the woman looked into the eyes of the girl.

There was a wonderful change about this woman. By a sort of miracle or rather by the divine hand of God she had lost her great misery and that which had made her hard, cruel, resentful, selfish, lay low and was in fact forgotten in a certain coffin underground, where her poor broken-down idol, a man unworthy of his name, who had found forgiveness and peace at the very end, slept that sleep which knows no waking.

The expression is perhaps incorrect, for while the body of this poor wayfarer, this poor waster of all life's good and beautiful things lay in his sheltered grave, his spirit, the only part of him worth thinking of, was far away.

What training Valentine Trent underwent in the better and the higher life it is not for us to say. But Elizabeth Beaufort had no doubt whatsoever on the subject.

"He was never a man while he lived," she was saying now to his mother, "but he is a man now. When next you meet him he will be worthy of your love and of—of Adrian's."

Mrs. Trent paused a moment to wipe away some tears.

"Now," said the girl, "You must keep up your heart. You must do what you promised Valentine to do. By the way I have seen the design for his grave. I think . is all sufficient. I think, in short, it is beautiful."

"You thought of it, Elizabeth, you are so wonderful."

"Well, you see," answered Elizabeth, "we cannot possibly say much and yet we can express a great deal."

"And what is the exact inscription?" faltered Mrs. Trent. "I—somehow—I dared not ask you."

"I have asked," said Elizabeth, "to have

put on the simple white cross the one word " VALENTINE."

"And beneath it the verse which I think you have lived up to.

" As one whom his mother comforteth."

Mrs. Trent gave a pathetic half-smothered cry.

But just then there came a cheery sound in the air—the sound of wheels, the gay tone of men's voices. Elizabeth felt herself turning deadly white. Mrs. Trent in her deep black struggled to get into the house, but Elizabeth held her firmly.

" Let us turn and meet the conqueror and the hero."

By this time her own cheeks were slightly flushed. Two men hurried across the dewy lawn. One was the governor of Hartleypool—the other Adrian Trent.

" Mother! mother!" he said, to the bowed down woman, and she allowed him to clasp her in his arms, and she felt the strength of his brave young presence and a surprised sense of rejoicing came over her for she knew that at long last she *loved him*. She loved him deeply, she loved him in that sort of way which no woman could ever forget or undo, which must remain with her and comfort her to the end of her days.

The white-haired governor stood a little

apart and Elizabeth also stood apart. Her face, was white again now, as white as her pretty dress, but her magnificent eyes were liquid with that feeling which is far too deep for tears.

Mrs. Trent took her son's hand and put it into the hand of Elizabeth.

"Children, I leave you," she said. "Only one thing before I go indoors. Captain Marshall, you will come with me perhaps. This girl has been to me as twenty daughters. Her love has been exceeding great. I cannot give her up, even if *you* can, Adrian, my boy, my dear boy."

The old man and the old lady went into the house together and now, in the dew-covered garden, there were two nightingales answering each other from tree to tree and there were two young people standing very close together, so close that at first they almost touched.

Then with a great cry, a cry of exceeding joy, Adrian Trent threw his arms round Elizabeth and swept her close, close, ever closer to his strong body.

"My prisoner," he said, "mine at last, mine for ever. Oh, God, you are good, you are good!"

"And you are *my* prisoner, best-beloved," she replied.

THE END

Lightning Source UK Ltd.
Milton Keynes UK
UKHW011957061118
331892UK00011B/1129/P